HALF-BREED

He cut a reed-slender figure in the grease-blackened buckskins of the frontier scout. The shirt and leggins were heavily fringed; the moccasins, flashily quilled and beaded.

He was long-armed and legged; his face, the mouth wide and cruel as any Cheyenne Dog Soldier's, was as angular and flint-keen as a lance blade.

He sat on his pony, a keg-headed, pot-bellied beast, Sioux-style, legs dangling straight down, back half bent, shoulders hunched forward. In the saddle scabbard under his knee snugged the latest spring-plate Winchester. Cross-belted over the hips, tied down at the thighs, two worn Colts rode low and handy.

For a Sioux-reared half-breed there was always trouble in the camps of the white man. This time Pawnee Perez was riding into a deadly noose of prejudice, ready to snap.

RED BLIZZARD
A NOVEL OF THE
NORTH PLAINS SIOUX

by Clay Fisher

RED BLIZZARD
*A Bantam Book | published by arrangement with
Clay Fisher*

PRINTING HISTORY
Simon and Schuster edition published 1951
Bantam edition | June 1971
2nd printing .... January 1981

ISBN 0–553–14542–8

Published simultaneously in the United States and Canada

---

*Bantam Books are published by Bantam Books, Inc. Its trade-
mark, consisting of the words "Bantam Books" and the por-
trayal of a bantam, is Registered in U.S. Patent and Trademark
Office and in other countries. Marca Registrada. Bantam
Books, Inc., 666 Fifth Avenue, New York, New York 10103.*

PRINTED IN THE UNITED STATES OF AMERICA

11 10 9 8 7 6 5 4 3 2

"Had Pawnee Perez been a white man, you would know his name as you do Custer's or Kit Carson's. But history has no use for half-breeds. . . ."

RED BLIZZARD

1 WASICUN

The White Man

CLANTON'S MEN WERE AS HARD AS THE BAKED EARTH UNDER
their rawhide infantry boots. Their eyes, peering red and
slitted from the alkali-stained masks of their faces, narrowed
yet more at the column of smoke towering black and greasy
there to the north beyond the Powder.

Funny about smoke. When you first got transferred out
to the Territory you didn't think much about smoke. Why
should you? You'd seen lots of it. You'd been with Sheridan
down in Georgia. You knew how a house or a barn or a
corncrib went up. You'd lain outside Petersburg for nine
months while Grant chomped his cigar at your buttside, and
you knew what crawled skyward after your artillery quieted
down to cool its throats. That was smoke, sure. But out here
in Wyoming it was different. After a few months out here
you began to "know" smoke. It got so it meant something
to you. Like maybe your life, for instance.

You got so you could look off across the plains at a fat,
white mushroom of smoke, and shrug, "Hell, prairie fire." You
got so you could gander out beyond the hills at that ash-gray
smoke with the orange flame stabbing its twisting undergut,
and have no more to say than, "Damned if they haven't fired
the brush again."

And you got so you could look up a long, hot valley like
this one you were marching up now, seeing that fat, black

1

smoke you were seeing now, and know what kind of smoke that was, too. And what you knew was that it wasn't grass smoke and that it wasn't brush smoke.

From the stunted cedar scrub atop the granite escarpment that shouldered the valley down which Clanton's troops were marching, a single pair of eyes peered long at the smoke column beyond the Powder, then shifted to watch that other column coming up the valley below. This other column was not fat and black like the smoke, but a thin, dust-dirty blue. It was not soft and billowing, either, but lean and tough as a tendon. This was a column of marching men, a column all the way from Fort Loring to the south, a wiry, fighting column, dirt-caked, red-eyed, bone-weary. These were regulars. No frontier militia of border rowdies, here. These were hard survivors of the War between the States, and they weren't probing northward up that rock-girt track for exercise or to broaden their cultural aspects.

Watching them from the escarpment, detailing every item of their identity, the chert-hard eyes above showed no emotion. No surprise, no fear, no relief. Certainly no gladness. Pawnee Perez knew better than to be glad to see white troops marching toward the Powder when Makhpiya Luta, the War Chief, had told them their crossing of that stream meant war.

Perez knew more. He knew, now, why that black smoke rolled to the north. An hour before he could only have told you *what* the smoke was. Now he could tell you *why.* Still, those were white men marching down there. They must be warned, and if Perez didn't warn them, nobody would. There weren't any white men left to do it. Perez knew that. It was up to him.

Not that the troops wouldn't guess what lay ahead of them under that reaching smoke spiral. They would also guess what circled the ground around that smoke. But what they wouldn't guess was *who* led the circle and *how many* rode in it. These were the things Perez knew, these were the things he had to tell them.

He knew these things because an hour before, the Winchester, now cold and quiet in his right hand, had been hot and noisy with hard firing. The two Colts, now silent in their strapped-down holsters, had been out and talking very loud. And the reason he had to tell them, those marching white men down there, of these things he knew, was because he, Pawnee Perez, was one of them. He was of their blood.

Perez slid back down off the granite ridge, pushing himself with slow movements of his free left hand. When he was down off the skyline he stood up and you saw him for the first time.

A dry, spare man, Pawnee Perez, better than six feet in height, clean and quick and furtive in movement. He went along behind the ridge toward his pony, his gait the ambling, reaching gait of the High Plains Sioux. His wide shoulders were bent forward in that permanent hunch peculiar to those who have spent their lives perpetually half crouched, ready to spring for cover and weapon at the first crack of a twig or hiss of a war arrow. His face was angular, high-cheekboned, low-foreheaded, the mouth as wide and cruel as the slash of a hunting knife.

Perez was a half-breed Pawnee, orphaned early, hard-reared among a succession of Sioux and Cheyenne war camps. In his teens, drawn to the side of the white man by the race-calling of his European father's blood, he had spent his early manhood learning and walking the trails of the *Wasicun*.

But the white way was a hard way for Pawnee Perez. The tracks of the *Wasicun* toed out, those of the *Shacun*, the Red People, toed in. There was always trouble in the camps of the white man for Perez—withal, the young Pawnee breed had fairly earned his reputation as the best wagon guide on the Virginia City Road. Perez knew, even as he started down to warn the soldier chiefs, that he was stepping into a deadly noose of prejudice, ready-set to snap around his corded, bronze neck.

Sioux-reared, fathered by a white Basque fur trader, mothered of a Pony Stealer squaw, the half-breed was a strange, friendless man with the fires of but one ambition burning in his dark breast: to belong, by force of achievement, to the white race of his father. Accordingly, though he went warily, he went unhesitatingly to warn the men below.

The larger of the two officers fronting the troop column raised his right hand, the yellow gauntlet flicking quickly right and left. The column stumbled to a halt, the officers sitting their horses, stirrup to stirrup, squinted gazes fixed on the distant smoke.

Colonel Travis Clanton was a barracks officer, an engineer by training, a martinet by inclination. He was a strict disciplinarian with a good military record as a brevet major general in the late war. He was a clean man, honest, open, friendly, and as much out of his element on the frontier as a trout in a dust puddle.

"What do you make of it?" he asked the smaller man.

Major Phil Stacey was his commander's antithesis. Short, red-bearded, imperious, Stacey was a cavalryman who rated himself, professionally, somewhere between Von Seydlitz and Tamerlane. "Wagons burning, naturally." His words were snappish, impatient.

"I suppose it's that train we sent the convoy after."

Stacey looked at his superior, his annoyance just shy of patent. "Yes, sir. Sergeant Stoker and eight mounted infantry. Your own men, Colonel." This last was deliberate but the older man seemed not to notice it, and Stacey concluded. "It's got to be that train. No other has gone up the Virginia City Road since Red Cloud sent you the warning at Fort Keene last week. You'll recall I asked you at the time to let me trail the train with fifty men." A pause here, then meaningfully, "At the time, Colonel, you were of the opinion that a sergeant and one squad could cut the detail nicely."

Again Colonel Clanton appeared oblivious to the plain criticism. "There were about twelve wagons, weren't there, Stacey?"

"Yes, a family train. Women, children, livestock. Going up to Montana to take land. If you remember, the wagon captain wouldn't wait for a convoy. Most of our troops were out on wood-cutting details and you couldn't spare him a squad for two days. At least that was your opinion. The captain said his wagon guide wanted to get on up the Road right away. Something about his having heard—the guide, that is—that Red Cloud was moving up onto the Virginia City Road so that he could stop any trains from getting past the Powder. The guide told the wagon captain that if they got through on the Virginia City Road it would have to be before Red Cloud got into position across it. The captain believed his story, apparently, deciding to try and beat the Sioux up the Road. You issued orders for them to wait but they went on ahead. I guess you remember."

"Yes"—the words were as level as the gaze that accompanied them—"I remember quite a few things you may not suppose I do, Major." Stacey shifted under the use of the military title. "I remember that train pulling into the fort. I remember two little girls sitting on the tailboard of a Pittsburgh. They had the yellowest curls and the shyest eyes I ever saw. I remember a young woman smiling at me and waving as they rode in. She was just a girl herself, no older than my daughter, Lura, but she had a baby in her arms and a blue-eyed toddler on the box beside her. I remember an imp of a boy, about ten, slouching by on a mule, snapping me a big grin and a proper salute. Some things I don't forget, Stacey." The words had softened for a moment, were suddenly honed with sharpness. "Who *was* the guide on that train, Stacey?"

"John Perez, a half-breed Pawnee. Raised by Red Cloud's Oglala, I understand. I don't know him and I didn't get to see him at the fort. He was out 'scouting' the Virginia City Road, uptrail. But I know his reputation and while there's nothing definite on him, folks just don't trust a half-breed guide in Sioux country. Particularly one brought up among the damn Oglala. You can't blame them, as I see it. In this case the train had to hire him on because it's near impossible to get a white guide to work north of Fort Loring since you had that pow-wow with Red Cloud and Man-Afraid-of-His-Horses down there this spring."

Stacey hesitated, his thin lips stiffening under the starch of sarcasm. "You remember that pow-wow, don't you, Colonel? Red Cloud called you 'The Little White Chief' and wanted to know what the hell you and all the Walk-a-Heaps were doing in this country, when the Grandfather in Washington had just promised the Red Brother to keep the white man out of the Powder River treaty lands."

"Yes"—the Colonel's words were beginning to show an edge of impatience—"and I also told him why we were here, didn't I?"

"You certainly did, sir, though you'll remember I advised against it."

"We won't go over that again," Clanton's voice was short. "I was given orders to come up here and build a fort forty miles north of Fort Keene and I'm going to do just that."

"Yes, sir"—Stacey's acceptance carried a question—"and while we're up here, what are we going to do about that smoke up ahead?"

"We'll go on up, of course. Nothing else we can do. When you see smoke it's already too late to do anything for the poor devils in that train."

"Too late to do anything for them, maybe," Stacey's words began to jump with excitement, "but how about the hostiles? There's a little something we can do for them!"

"Such as?" A martinet, perhaps, but no utter fool, Colonel Clanton.

5

"Colonel, let me take the horses and go on up ahead of you. We might just catch the red buzzards hanging around snapping their beaks."

"Out of the question, I think. These are infantry. They're not your cavalry, Stacey. They're no good on a horse, you know that. Besides, you've got mounts for only thirty men."

"I could ride through the whole damn Sioux Nation with fifty!" The red-bearded officer's harsh claim was delivered with that brand of conviction which comes in packages labeled "Caution—Pure Ignorance!"

"I don't know, Stacey, I—"

"Colonel, let me go on up. There can't be many of them this close to us. They wouldn't dare operate in force so near Fort Keene. It's probably a raiding party down from the north, not even aware of our presence. Hunkpapas, I'd guess. We know Crazy Horse is in the Black Hills and we know, now, that Perez was lying about Red Cloud coming up this way. At least, we suspect he was. Let's say both Crazy Horse and Red Cloud are ruled out, anyway. Who does that leave? Damn it, Colonel, if you'll just let me—"

Clanton's interruption still held strong question. "Stacey, that train had about twenty men in it plus a tough, experienced guide and nine regular soldiers. We are forced to assume, now, that this train and all those men are gone. It would have taken a strong force to wipe them out, don't you think?"

"Well, yes and no, but not necessarily, sir. Look at it this way." Stacey had the "Indian itch," that crazy disease so common to green frontier officers, wherein the prime symptom is the convinced delusion that a squad of regulars could handle any one whole tribe of hostiles. The knowledge that his superior didn't share his ailment caused the major to choose his words carefully. "They probably hit the train when it was noon-halted, maybe even with the teams spanned out and grazing. Another thing. Let's not overlook this guide's background. Blood is thicker than a wagon scout's pay, especially red blood. You know that. What about this half-breed guide leading the train into a set trap? That was a fat train. Lots of livestock, good weapons, big mules, plenty of horses."

"By God, you may be right." The thought of a plotted ambush involving treachery on the half-breed guide's part had not occurred to the phlegmatic Clanton. "Go on up, Stacey, but keep your flankers wide and if you run into the hostiles in force, retire back on me. I mean stay clear of them if you see more than a hundred of them. That's a direct order. You're straight on it, now?"

"Yes, sir!" The younger officer's answer hopped with eagerness, but in wheeling his horse to return to the resting column, a frown whipped across his face. "Now, what the devil?" His scowling glance was directed, with his question, upvalley.

Following his gaze, Clanton, too, saw the approaching horseman.

Watching the stranger come up, the two officers saw a reed-slender figure in the grease-blackened buckskins of the frontier scout. The shirt and leggins were heavily fringed; the moccasins, flashily quilled and beaded. The man rode bareheaded, his lank hair hanging shoulder-long and straight. He was long-armed and legged; his face, the mouth wide and cruel as any Cheyenne Dog Soldier's, was as angular and flint-keen as a lance blade. He sat his pony, a keg-headed, pot-bellied beast, Sioux-style, legs dangling straight down, back half bent, shoulders hunched forward. In the saddle scabbard under his knee snugged the latest, spring-plate Winchester. Cross-belted over the hips, tied down at the thighs, two worn Colts rode low and handy. He drew up to them making the palms-out sign of peace.

Stacey returned the sign but the scout ignored him, addressing Clanton instead.

It was now you got your second surprise about Pawnee Perez. From the looks of him you'd be ready for any kind of voice but the one you heard. True, it had the male timbre you'd expect from a figure of such ferinity, but otherwise it fooled you. It was as soft as a woman's, gentle as a drawing master's.

"*Hau.* I'm John Perez."

In his astonishment that any such figure could turn out to be the suspected wagon guide, Clanton forgot to return the inevitable "*hau*" of prairie protocol, stammering, instead, "Perez! Pawnee Perez, the wagon guide?"

"And an evil-looking bastard if I ever saw one," interpolated Stacey, evenly, before adding, his stare as challenging as the question, "Where the hell have you been, half-breed, and what's happened to your train?"

The coffee-skinned scout looked at him a long three seconds before deliberately and slowly turning to face Clanton. "Colonel, my train's gone. Everybody in it wiped out."

The column commander just looked at him, unable to match

7

the low, clear English with the savage Sioux looks and evil half-breed reputation.

"I suppose you're just lucky!" broke in Stacey, stung by the scout's calculated ignoring of him. "We'll sure as hell be interested in knowing how you got away while everybody else was wiped out!"

This time Perez didn't even give him the weight of a look. "It was partly my fault," he went on, talking to Clanton. "I made a bad guess."

"Worse than you've got any idea," growled Stacey. "You're in a tight, Indian."

"Did my soldiers catch up with you?" Clanton, too, ignored his fellow officer.

"Yes, Colonel, they did. Sundown last night. A sergeant and eight men. They died like men, especially the sergeant. Him and me was the last ones left. He rid out with me when the others was all done fer. When they shot his hoss out from under him, the sergeant flopped down behind him and kept firin' to cover my getaway. *Woyuonihan. Wagh.* He was plenty man. I jest kept on goin'."

"Oh, naturally!" Stacey showed his teeth. "You wouldn't be expected to stay and die like a white man."

"That'll do, Stacey. Let's not convict this man before we've heard him. We haven't got him on a drumhead court-martial and we're not interested in his pedigree."

"My father was white!" said Perez, and that was all he said.

Colonel Clanton started to question the newcomer further, but Stacey interrupted. "Colonel, I'll go along up ahead, now. Do you want me to put this man under arrest before I leave?"

"No, I'll talk to him a bit, yet."

"Good. Well, I'll move on up ahead. See if I can't catch me a few of our guest's little red friends still watching the bonfire."

"I wouldn't, if I was ye. Ye won't git back." The scout's observation was easy-drawled but it hit Stacey across the face like the haft of a war-ax.

"What the hell do you mean?" The major shouldered his horse into the stranger's pony, thrusting his red-bearded jaw up toward the tall rider's face.

"I mean thar's upwards of four hunderd Sioux ridin' a victory gallop around them wagon embers, right now."

"Four hundred!" Incredulity spiked Clanton's exclamation.

8

"Impossible!" snorted Stacey, simultaneously.

"Closer to four hunderd and fifty," went on the tall half-breed, "mostly Oglala Bad Faces. And under a pretty piss-cuttin' chief."

"What chief?" This from Stacey, rasping with pugnacity.

"Makhpiya Luta."

"And who the goddam hell is Makhpiya Luta? I never heard of him."

"Oh, I reckon mebbe ye have, Major." The breed's black eyes appeared to slit still more as they fastened on the irascible Stacey. "Only most likely ye call him 'Red Cloud.'"

"Red Cloud?" Again Clanton was incredulous, his methodical mind jogging along on legs too short to pace the conversation.

"The real article," offered Perez with a shrug. "The one and only."

"That's a damn lie!" Stacey was livid now. "Colonel, Red Cloud wouldn't dare pull such an attack. By God, not even if he *was* up here on the Road, he wouldn't dare. And by the way," here whirling quickly on Perez, "weren't you the bright guide who said Red Cloud *wasn't* up here, yet? Weren't you the smart boy who was going to get that train up the Virginia City Road before Red Cloud *did* get up here, providing he was coming?" Stacey turned eagerly to his superior. "How about that, Colonel? You remember me telling you what this half-breed told the wagon captain, don't you? That Red Cloud was coming but that they could beat him up the Road if they left right away? Right away, that is, before we could spare an escort for the train."

"Yes," the colonel's words were slow, "how about that, Perez? It doesn't look right, at all. You can see that, I hope."

"I kin see it all right. I could see it before I come down to warn ye, but it's like I told ye. I made a sour guess. I had a hunch and it clabbered up on me, that's all." The softness of the scout's tones failed to cushion the bitterness in them. "I had information thet the War Chief was comin', but thet he was five suns east. I know, now, thet information stunk as high as a salmon six days in the sun. It come from an Injun and God knows I ain't got any excuse fer not knowin' Injuns by this time. I told ye I allowed this wipe-out was part my fault. Well, I'm still sayin' it. I fell fer a bait. They got me into a *wickmunke*—that's their word fer 'trap'—and then they jest nacherally give it to me, both jaws. That's all."

9

"You'd be lucky if it was," Stacey's comment was acid, "but I don't think 'that's all' by any means. I think there's plenty more to come. How about it, Colonel?"

"I'm afraid Major Stacey is right, Perez." Clanton spoke thoughtfully. "You must see it doesn't look right, from our view, for you to get out clean, the sole survivor, on a bad wipe-out like this. Especially, you being a half-blood and reared, I'm told, by the same Oglala you claim did this massacre. I don't know, man. You admittedly went up the Road in what appeared to us an unreasonable hurry. In fact, you went up against my express orders to wait for an escort. Stacey"—here turning to the major—"Perez was informed of that order, wasn't he?"

"Not in person. I told the wagon captain. Perez was up the Road, 'scouting' at the time. We know, now, what he really was doing was chinning with his Sioux relatives about their dirty *wickmunke.*"

"Perez, did the wagon captain tell you about my order?"

"He did."

"And you advised him to go on up the Road, anyway? Against my orders? Without a guard?"

"Yeah, I told the wagon captain thar was only two things to do: go ahead, fast, or turn back to Fort Loring and go out the old Oregon Road. Wal, it's gittin' into autumn, Colonel. They had no time to go back. Early snow could have caught them, bad, in the high country. Sech as the choice was, they tooken it theirse'fs."

"Oh, horse crap!" barked Stacey. "It's a bald-assed lie and he knows there's no way to prove out on him, one way or another. Colonel, I'm charging this half-red bastard with deliberately steering that train into a trap. That's flat, sir."

Clanton still hesitated. There was that in the manner and soft speech of the breed which didn't quite tally with his dark, alien look and the lethal charge Stacey was loading onto him. Seeing the hesitation, the major spurred in with his usual hard ride. "Look at this man, sir. According to him, he's just ridden and fought through four hundred of the toughest hostiles on the North Plains, and by God, Colonel, you find me one mark of it on him!"

Clanton, old-line Army indecision apparent in every halting word, nodded. "Yes, it's rather stiff to believe a man could come through all that without a scratch to show for it. What do you say, Perez?"

The scout shrugged, his lean face flushing. "I've spoke my piece. I ain't got nothin' to add onto it."

Stacey now moved in abruptly. "Colonel, this man clearly got away from that train *before* it was attacked. I say put him under arrest."

Colonel Clanton looked at the half-breed scout, steadily, regret plainly evident in his ensuing agreement. "Perez, I'm afraid there's no other course. You're under arrest; the charge, murder and complicity in inciting hostile Indians to attack peaceful white civilians." The breed stared at the back of his pony's ears, his wide mouth hard-clamped as any Oglala's. Watching him a moment, Clanton concluded, his words dropping like sleet on dry ground, "In any event you know what the sentence will be if you're convicted—you'll go to the Dry Tortugas for life."

Perez said nothing, gave no sign he'd even heard the column commander. Clanton shifted uncomfortably, added lamely, "I'm not saying you are guilty. I'm not even saying I, personally, think or feel you are. But the circumstances are impossible. Do you understand that?"

"Yeah, sure." The narrow face held no visible emotion. "I allow I knowed all about thet before I rid down hyar to warn ye."

"He's a hero! Can't you see that, Colonel?" Stacey's short laugh was a sneer set to mirth.

"My father was white," said Pawnee Perez.

Colonel Travis Clanton was a big man, precise, unhumorous, cautious. A West Pointer, he fought his wars by the book. He was not forgetting, now, that the book said, "When in doubt, go slow." And the more he thought of Pawnee Perez, the more in doubt he was.

When the scout had ridden in with his implausible report on the burning of his wagon train by Red Cloud and the Oglala Bad Faces, the colonel had at once remanded his order permitting Stacey to take the mounted troop forward. He had then thrown the entire company into a tight security camp. "We'll stay right here until morning," he'd told Stacey. "At that time we'll see what develops. Meantime, you and Captain Benson get the camp set for trouble. I want double flankers out at one hundred and three hundred yards. And no fires after dark. I don't want to see any rifles stacked, either, or any stock grazing off-picket. When you've got everything in order, get Benson and come up here to my tent. We've still got that young fool, Collins, and my daughter to worry about, you know. And send Perez up here. I want to question him some more."

Now, with dusk coming in fast and the cooking fires winking out across the camp, Clanton was ready for his renewed talk with the half-breed. The column commander instinctively liked the scowling Pawnee breed, just as Major Stacey apparently held an intuitive distrust of him. Still, the man's story was thin as April grass, leaving Stacey's sharp accusations largely unanswered.

Looking at the prisoner where he squatted dour and silent across the small fire that still guttered before the command tent, Colonel Clanton wondered what ideas were flicking past behind the narrow, black windows of those hard eyes.

In his turn, Perez was sizing up the officer, but with more luck. He felt sorry for Clanton but his sympathy was tempered with the bright steel of realism which alloyed all his own thinking and character.

Perez had been born on this frontier and had sucked hard at its dry breasts. His weanling years had been spent with his mother's people, his knowledge of the Indian way of seeing and doing things hence being a very real one.

In point of fact he had never known his mother, a raiding party of Cheyennes having literally ripped the cradleboard which bore him from her back. Subsequently he'd been traded back and forth after the Indian custom with captive children, from tribe to tribe, so, as he approached manhood, he'd lived with no less than five of the hostile prairie tribes, including both Red Cloud's Oglala and Tatanka Yotanka's, Sitting Bull's, Hunkpapa Sioux, as well as the Cheyenne peoples of Dull Knife and Two Moons. Through all this wandering, since the Indian tribal descent is a matriarchal one, he had retained the identity of his maternal origin. Among the Sioux he was thus called, literally, Little Pony Stealer; the Pawnees being called the Pony Stealer People after their brilliantly earned reputation as the premier horse thieves of the prairies.

No matter that maturity had made of Perez a six-foot-plus warrior, reared in the flint-brittle Sioux and Cheyenne traditions, he remained, simply, "Little" Pony Stealer. Through his subsequent associations with the whites as scout and wagon guide through the forbidden realms of his dangerous foster parents, he'd picked up the shorter, if less poetic title, of "Pawnee."

12

Looking at Colonel Clanton, now, the scout's red past let him see the man with a judgment almost factual in its deductions. The Indian learns one thing if nothing else: to read the nature of a man or an animal, quickly and unerringly.

Perez saw a big man across the fire from him. A clean man, decent and honest, slow with caution in both manner and fact. A broad forehead topped a wide-open pair of blue eyes. His nose was short, mouth relaxed, chin wide and clean-shaven. His skin was very white, the kind that prairie-burns continually, never browning up. His age, Perez guessed, was about forty-five. He was obviously by nature too soft for the frontier, by training too set in the tradition of white military supremacy. The thought crossed the scout's mind, as he sat waiting for the colonel to speak, that the White Soldier Chiefs in Washington couldn't have picked a man better suited to lead troops into Red Cloud's country—and into disaster.

"Perez," Clanton began, "I could put more faith in your story if I knew something about you. Will you talk to me before Major Stacey and Captain Benson show up? As your people say, 'my tongue is straight and my heart is good toward you.'"

The half-breed studied the officer a moment, then nodded. This Eagle Chief spoke the truth. A man could tell that. His heart was indeed good. To this one, any man could talk, even a half-breed. Briefly, Perez sketched his life, concluding with a statement put forward to be taken or left just as it was. "So thet's the way it's bin, Colonel. From the time I was about seventeen and found out from a wanderin' oldster of my mother's tribe thet my father had bin a Basque fur trader named John Perez, and thet he had had the Black Robe marry him and my mother, I've regarded myse'f as a white man. And I've near broke my butt tryin' to be one. Don't ask me why, fer I cain't tell ye. Thar's jest somethin' to bein' white thet puts a man above an Injun, I guess. Leastaways, I want to be white and I aim to be if I kin make it. Right now, it don't look like I kin."

Pausing, the gaunt breed raised his glittering eyes to stare at Clanton. "All along, I've called myse'f John Perez and said I'm white. But the Injuns call me Little Pony Stealer and say I'm red, while the whites call me Pawnee and say I'm a goddam breed."

"When I asked you if you'd talk to me," Clanton frowned, "I had in mind you might want to tell me something about the massacre this afternoon."

13

"Ye said ye wanted to know somethin' about me. Now I've told ye, and ye're like all the rest of the *Wasicun*. Ye don't believe it."

"I believe you, Perez, but what you've told me has no bearing on the charges we've got you under arrest for. Do you think it has?"

Perez looked into the fire. "Yeah," he nodded, shortly, "it has. I told ye about my Injun blood," here the ore of the half-breed's voice flashed the first thin stringer of iron-bearing malice, "because I know damn well the reason I'm under arrest ain't because my train was burnt."

Clanton furrowed his brow, waited a minute, spoke sharply. "I don't follow you, Perez. You say we don't have you under arrest because of the massacre? Let me ask you a question. Just what the devil do we have you under arrest for?"

The scout, in turn, waited before answering. "Let *me* ask *you* a question, Colonel," his strange voice purred, powder-soft as the fall of a moccasin in deep trail dust. "If the guide on thet train had been a white man would ye have arrested him on sight, like you done me?"

Clanton flushed, started to stammer, stopped in mid-sputter, announced manfully, "Damn it all, I don't suppose I would have, Perez, but where does that get us?"

"It gits us right whar we are now," said Perez, quietly. "I'm a half-blood Injun and I cain't he'p it. Ye've arrested me because I *am* part Injun and I guess ye cain't he'p thet, but I want ye to hear this, Colonel Clanton." The black eyes sparkled like chipped obsidian as the soft voice purred upward to a plane of hard vibrancy. "I didn't lead thet train into thet ambush and ye're not goin' to send me to Florida fer it." He paused a minute, dropping his tones back to the old quietness. "I saw every man, woman and child in thet train die. When they was all dead and thar was still a chancet to save my own life, I tooken it. I'm a Pawnee breed, not a hero. I did whut I could and then got out. My tongue's bin straight and I'm through talkin'."

Perez was a literal man, Clanton being unable to get another word out of him. He was still trying when Benson and Stacey came up. The three officers began at once to discuss their situation.

The nature of that discussion, the pale-skinned, gray-eyed, flame-haired nature of it, lifted a last desperate hope before the narrowed eyes of the listening prisoner.

The captive sat by unnoticed, apparently unnoticing, but

when the conversation introduced the predicament of the heretofore-mentioned Lieutenant Collins, Perez swung his head instantly to the group by the fire. Here, perhaps, lay his one chance to escape trial for the ambush, with its certain sentence to the Tortugas. Perez had seen too many Sioux disappear after summary Army trials not to know that his own fate hung in the snare of the officers' quiet words. He listened intently while Clanton talked.

"Naturally, our first consideration is the men"—the colonel dropped his words hesitantly, as a man will when he is trying to tie the tail of emotion on the kite of duty—"but you both know my daughter, Lura, and will therefore understand my feeling in this situation."

"No one could fail to, sir!" It was youthful Captain Winslow Benson, doing his blond best to sound more than his twenty-three years. "Your only child and—"

"And," interrupted Stacey, feelingly, "the most beautiful girl I ever saw!" The aspirations of Phil Stacey in the direction of the colonel's daughter were well publicized, and certainly well inspired. The girl had visited the garrison at Fort Loring six months before, taking every commissioned heart in Wyoming Territory back to Missouri with her.

"Thank you," nodded Clanton, quietly. "Our problem remains to decide the probable whereabouts of Collins' troop and the possibilities we have of contacting them, always considering our own doubtful position, of course."

"I suppose the damn fool's lost." Stacey's bitterness was compounded by thoughts of Lura being alone with a dashing second lieutenant of cavalry. "Good God, we ask for six troops of cavalry and they send us one. And that one under a wet-nosed shavetail who couldn't find his way to the ladies' latrine without a compass and two scouts. When was he supposed to report, anyway?"

"A week ago." The gravity of the statement was etched in the frown-lines on Clanton's usually smooth forehead. "The last we heard was the telegraph report from Muleshoe Creek, saying he had Lura with him and was starting for Fort Keene the next day."

"That's a hundred and fifty miles south of here," asserted Captain Benson, trying once more to sound as terse and competent as Stacey. "Something must have happened."

Stacey gave him the compliment of a sneer, and for the moment there was no more talk.

While the officers squatted, wordless, Perez' agile mind was

15

riding itself to a yellow-lather gallop. The mention of the colonel's daughter had thrown the spurs of desperation into the flanks of his searching thoughts. If he could somehow convince Clanton that he, Perez, could guide any possible relief column to the lost Lieutenant Collins, there might yet be a bobtailed chance of cutting his stick the hell away from the clearly forecast free trip to the Tortugas that that goddam little red-bearded Major Stacey had talked Colonel Clanton into handing him. By God, it just might work. The thing was to get the commander to send out a small relief party right away, tonight. Then, in the darkness of the downtrail journey, with Pawnee Perez in the lead, guiding, many things might happen—

Clanton's solemn conclusion interrupted the half-breed scout's quick-forming plan. "Our problem, now, is to decide what we're going to do about finding Collins in view of what we know about Red Cloud being out in force."

"What you've been told by that stinking half-breed, you mean!" interjected Stacey.

Colonel Clanton looked at his junior, closely. "I don't think I care for your attitude, Phil. I'll ask you to watch yourself. I've talked with Perez rather carefully and I see no reason to doubt his report on Red Cloud. The fact is, gentlemen, I'm a bit inclined to believe his entire story. At any rate there's little point in obviating the precariousness of our own position, and that of Collins and my girl, by prejudice based in this man's failure to be a European."

Stacey bowed his head to the fire, locking his teeth, hard, so that only the proper words would escape them. "Yes, sir. What's your suggestion, Colonel?"

"We'll break camp in the morning, as soon as it's clear Red Cloud doesn't intend attacking us. We'll backtrail until we contact Collins. I don't see another course at the moment, gentlemen. Unless a better suggestion is forthcoming, that's it."

Neither Benson nor Stacey seemed to have such a suggestion but one came nevertheless, and from a forgotten quarter.

"I've got a better suggestion, Colonel." The purring voice of Perez fell across the little group, easing down in the silence-hole lingering after Clanton's announcement.

"Oh, for Christ's sake—" began Stacey, Clanton cutting him short.

"Go ahead, Perez. Let's hear your suggestion."

The scout talked quickly, earnestly. "First off, Red Cloud

won't attack this column. Thet's absolute. He ain't ready fer any sech big medicine. He sure aims to drive ye whites out'n the Powder River country, but his big attack won't come till this winter, along after the fall buffalo hunt's over, the meat's all in and dried, and a big white wind comes blowin'."

"What the hell do you mean, 'a big white wind'?" Stacey eyed the half-breed suspiciously.

"Blizzard," shrugged Perez. "They love to operate under a blizzard. Snow raises hell with the Army and don't hamper a Sioux no more'n a noseful of snot."

Stacey lost patience. "Colonel, what's the use of listening to this Indian talk? White winds! Buffalo hunts! Meat drying! My ass! This red bastard's tongue is as crooked as a cavalry paymaster. We can't act on a word he says. Why—"

"Major Stacey, your attitude is commendably alert, but I happen to resent your profane speech. And I want to hear what this man has to say. Now, with your permission, sir—"

Stacey took his reprimand with a bristling "I beg your pardon, Colonel Clanton," and Perez continued.

"Ye've got too much force in this column fer Red Cloud to monkey with." The half-breed sensed that Clanton was really listening to him, thinking hard about what he was saying. Hope for the success of his plan grew. "He ain't the War Chief of the Seven Tribes fer nothin'. Ye'll hear a lot of commotion about some of the other chiefs, like Man-Afraid and Sitting Bull, but Red Cloud's different. He's a crazy kind of a Injun, moody, spooky, proud as a big bull elk with six strange cows."

"What the hell are you getting at?" Stacey's question was defiant. Perez continued, ignoring him.

"He told ye down to Fort Loring whut he'd do if ye come up hyar. Well, he'll do it. The next time ye hear from Red Cloud'll be when he lifts yer hair and runs off yer hosses. He's th'ough talkin'."

Clanton's interruption labored with his usual bear-like speed. "I don't see precisely what you're getting at, myself, Perez. You just told us he wouldn't attack us. Now it sounds like you're telling us he will. What *do* you mean?"

"Jest this. Red Cloud won't attack yer strong column of regulars. But ye say ye've got a green lieutenant and forty replacement Pony Soldiers runnin' around 'thout a wet nurse. In fact, lost sommers betwixt hyar and Fort Keene. And with yer own young daughter with them."

"Yes, that's right. Lieutenant Wilke Collins and G Troop

of the Eighth, up from Fort Loring. My daughter telegraphed she was coming up to Fort Keene with them. Thank God Murphy and Moriarity are along."

"Who're they?"

"Two regular sergeants."

"Wal, thet helps. But forty green Pony Soldiers and a damp-crotch lieutenant jest make a potlatch boiled to a turn fer Red Cloud and four hunderd Oglala Bad Faces. A white girl, daughter of the Little White Soldier Chief, won't slow their slobberin' down any, neither."

"So?" Colonel Clanton's query was strained.

"So, what do ye think Red Cloud will do to·git his paws on the daughter of the Soldier Chief who has broken the Fort Loring Treaty and come marchin' north of the Powder?"

"Well?" Clanton couldn't seem to get the picture. Perez, feeling his chance of scaring the Army leader into sending out a night column slipping away, fired his getaway load.

"Wal, lessen ye want Lieutenant Collins and his forty to jine Sergeant Stoker and his eight, ye'd best find him right now. Break camp and start back tonight. Send Major Stacey and those thirty mounted infantry on ahaid. Don't waste twelve hours sittin' hyar waitin' fer Red Cloud. He ain't comin'. But"—the scout's eyes gleamed suddenly slant and black—"he may be goin'. And whar he may be goin' is after yer new lieutenant. And yer daughter. This hyar whole coun-try is bellybutton-deep in hostiles. It's nigh impossible thet some scout band won't git their noses up Collins' butt. When they do, they'll have the War Chief down on top of him like a travois-load of hot, red rocks." The lean breed's last words were ominous. "Yer only chancet to save yer daughter is to beat Red Cloud to her. And yer only chancet to beat him to her is to let me guide the mounted relief column."

Clanton nodded. "You may underestimate Collins and over-figure the hostiles, Perez, but I see your point. I've half a mind to let you—"

"I can see his point, too!" burst in Stacey. "But not the one you see, Colonel. Sir, I think this lousy redskin is trying to get us to break camp and go into a night march for the simple purpose of getting us strung out for his friend Red Cloud to jump in the dark. The whole thing points that way, sending us out ahead of the column, you following, out of contact, his guiding the lead group—"

"By damn, Stacey, you may be right!" Apparently the possibility had not occurred to the colonel. Encouraged, the young officer swung hard at the suspected scout. Perez saw his chances going like an unhooked trout into deep water.

"Not only am I right, Colonel, but I suggest we all remember this man is under suspicion of one ambush already, and that he, himself, is one-half red Indian."

"Good Lord, yes," breathed Benson, fervently. "Let's not let him walk *us* into one, too!"

"Exactly my point!" snapped Stacey.

"All right." Clanton's voice was tired with finality. "We stay here as planned. Stacey, you and Benson check the outposts. See that every man not on picket or patrol is sleeping on his rifle. Perez, you—" Here the colonel's orders broke in mid-delivery, his glance widening as it fell on the half-breed scout. For the first time Perez heard his tones go sharp. "Dammit, man, what the devil's ailing you, now?"

Perez paid no attention to the question. He was half rolled on his side, his bound arms awkwardly twisted behind him. His head lay on the ground, right ear flat-pressed to the bare earth. Clanton started repeating his question but Perez raised his heard, snarling, "Shet up! All of ye. Be quiet!"

The three officers looked at one another in surprise. Stacey, laughing with nervous quickness, muttered something which sounded like "Insolent goddam Sioux bastard—" His words were lost in the thick silence which wrapped up the scout's abrupt command.

"What is it?" Clanton, leaning forward, made his whisper sound like a shout.

"Three, mebbeso four, hosses. Yeah, four. Comin' this way. Were runnin', now they're walkin'. Barefoot ponies." He lifted his head, rolling his body back to a sitting position. "Tell yer downvalley pickets to hold their fire. Don't leave them go blastin' up the landscape. Them are Injuns comin' in."

Captain Benson ran off to alert the pickets. "Shall we douse the fire?" Colonel Clanton's question was openly put to the bound prisoner.

"Naw. Thar's only four of them. Nobody with them. Hold up and see whut they want. They ain't blunderin' into ye, ye kin bet on thet. They know ye're hyar and they want somethin'."

Out of the darkness, downvalley, came a sudden calling-out of voices. Colonel Clanton could recognize Benson's voice in

19

challenge, but the answering tongue was a strange, guttural one. He didn't place it as Sioux, the only hostile language with which he was at all familiar.

"Cheyenne," vouchsafed the copper-skinned prisoner, "and if I remember thet voice, ye've got big company." A moment later Clanton heard the sibilant intake of Perez' breath. "Bigger then I thought, by God!" breathed the scout.

The figures of four mounted Indians loomed out of the blackness beyond the fire-glow. In their lead rode an old chief, very dark-skinned, ramrod-straight, long, braided hair as beautifully silver-gray as an old boar badger's roach. A single, black eagle feather, worn vertically at the back, Cheyenne-wise, adorned the braids. From the high choker of five-inch bear claws which circled his neck to the extravagantly beaded moccasins of white elk which cased his feet, every lineament of the old man's body and bearing bespoke the savage patrician, the nomad commander, the hereditary chief.

"That's Dull Knife," Perez side-mouthed his words to Clanton, never taking his eyes from the approaching warriors, "the stiff-backed old bird in front, the one with the black feather and the claw necklace. He's *the* Cheyenne chief." To the red men now drawn up sitting their ponies, tight-mouthed, outside the fire's light, the scout addressed a more formal comment. Rising gracefully, despite his bound arms, he inclined his head deferentially toward the old man.

"*Woyuonihan*," he said, using the Sioux greeting-word of respect for the warrior of reputation. "My father will forgive it that I cannot touch my brow. As you see—" Perez left the statement up in the air, ending it with an explanatory shrug of his pinioned arms, concluding, "The Little White Soldier Chief bids me tell you '*Hohahe*,' welcome to his tipi."

Turning to Clanton, the scout added, "I told him we respect such a great chief and thet he and his friends are welcome in yer tent."

The colonel nodded, smiling at Dull Knife, half raising his palm as he hesitatingly announced, "Uh, er, how. How, Chief!"

"*Hau!*" grunted the Cheyenne, without changing expression by so much as a nerve twitch. The other three savages sat as he did, graven, red gargoyles under the feeble lances of the restless fire.

Clanton shifted uncomfortably, glancing at Perez for help. Stacey for once held his tongue while Benson, who had come up behind the chiefs, stuttered, "The-the old man, the chief, I mean," indicating Dull Knife, "he can speak English. He said he wanted to talk to the Eagle Chief."

"Well, who the devil's the Eagle Chief?" Clanton's voice was shaded with the annoyance that always accompanies embarrassment.

It was then, had you been watching, you'd have seen the third strange thing about Perez—his smile. It was rare and bright, that smile, as fleeting and warm as a sunburst past the hard edge of a coming storm front. It ran over the clouding of his expression like summer lightning shooting the dark face of a thunderhead. Then it was gone just as quickly, seeming, again like lightning, to leave the scene of its passing darker than ever. You caught the instant flash of the snow-clean teeth back of the hard mouth, the sudden lambency of the piercing eyes in their immobile mask, and that was all. After that the face went dead again.

"Why, Colonel," he responded to Clanton's broadcast query, "thet's ye, sir. Ye're the Eagle Chief. They call ye thet from yer shoulder-eagles, jest like they call yer friend, General Crook, 'Three Stars.' "

"Well, what does he want?" asked Clanton, haltingly.

"Ye kin talk to him, direct. He savvies English. But first it would be a good idee"—the scout's words dropped to a tiptoe—"to shake hands with him. They love to shake hands."

Squaring his shoulders, the colonel stepped toward the motionless Cheyenne. Perez walked with him, calling out slowly, "This is the Little White Soldier Chief, Colonel Clanton. His eagles have seen much war and they are watchin' ye, now."

Dull Knife and his companions sat, impassive, not furnishing a face-muscle flutter among them. Indicating the famous Cheyenne with as much of a flourish as his bonds would permit, Perez announced, dramatically, "Dull Knife, head of the Cheyenne Nation, War Chief of all the Cut Arm People!" This was the Indians' name for the Cheyenne, taken from the latter's habit of cutting off the left arm or hand of their victims.

Clanton put out his right hand, uncertainly, being amazed when the old chief at once hopped down off his pony, seized the extended member, pumped it furiously. "Haul Haul Haul" he barked, his shy grin more suited to an Agency schoolboy than to the War Chief of all the Cheyennes.

"How," Clanton returned the greeting stiffly, meanwhile

trying to retrieve his hand from the windmilling the old Indian was giving it. "You are welcome in my camp."

Dull Knife's companions now dismounted to stand in turn for handshakes from the Eagle Chief. The first one to follow the wrinkled leader was another oldster, a patient-faced chief, short of stature, plainly dressed. Perez meant to see that this one didn't suffer, by comparison to Dull Knife, in his introduction.

"Two Moons," the scout was practically shouting, "a great chief, a famous horse thief!"

So far none of the Indians had given Perez any recognition, but at his reference to the old chief's horse-lifting talents, Two Moons turned to the scout with a wry smile. "From Little Pony Stealer this is high praise. *Waghl* But, indeed, let us say no more about it." He spoke in Cheyenne, Perez answering in the same tongue.

"Do not worry, Uncle. The Eagle Chief doesn't know you are the one who ran off his horse herd down at Fort Loring this spring."

"Aye, but he will if you do not put a hobble on that wagging tongue of yours. You chatter more than a young squaw after her first stabbing."

"He knows no Cheyenne, Uncle," Perez reassured him.

"Maybe not," broke in one of the two chiefs still waiting to be introduced, "but he will have time to learn it if you and old Two Moons are going to stand there all night with your tongues flying loose on both ends."

"Even so, my brother," nodded Perez, in serious acknowledgment of the breach in Courtesy Rules. "Let us get on with this business."

As he turned to Clanton, the latter queried brusquely, "What's going on, Perez? What are you talking about?"

The scout shrugged aside the questions, saying the chiefs were wrangling over the order of introduction. Quickly, he presented Red Arm and Black Horse, both well-known fighting chiefs in the prime of manhood. The two powerful Cheyenne now applied the considerable vigor of that primeness to the Eagle Chief's right arm.

"Damn it, Perez," the colonel's complaint held obvious appeal, "how long does this go on? I won't be able to use this arm for a week, now."

A gleam sparked the scout's eye. Speaking in Cheyenne, he addressed the visitors. "The Eagle Chief says he loves to shake hands with his red brothers but that he does not want all the joy for himself. He says the Oak Leaf Chief," pivoting here with a sweeping bow to the frowning Stacey, "would rather shake hands than eat young dog!"

"*Haul Haul Haul*" called out the Indians, descending greedily on the major.

"Damn you, Perez," he began, backing with such haste as to step squarely into the fire, "you red son of a bitch, I'll—" But by this time Major Phil Stacey's self-possession was as singed as his roasted buttside. The chiefs, having seized both his hands, two on each member, now stood pumping heartily, uttering an unbroken string of "*Haus*" as they worked Stacey's captive arms. The major wasn't man enough to stand up to the punishment. Face fuming, flank smoldering, he fought a successful retirement, ending up safely behind Clanton, both arms at last free of Indians, both, luckily, still in their sockets.

While the Cheyenne had been hand-pumping Clanton's junior around the fire, Perez had addressed the colonel briefly. "Happen ye might think they're playful by nature I kin assure ye they ain't. They're puttin' on the friendly act fer a reason. My guess is they've got somethin' unfriendly to say and want to git ye clear on how powerful good their hearts are before they spring it." Perez' opinion was no sooner given than proved out.

Leaving the red-faced Stacey as abruptly as they'd attacked him, the Cheyenne stalked over to the fire, seating themselves cross-legged before it, with scrupulous attention to the order of the sitting. "Ye kin allus tell Injun power by the way they set to a fire fer council," Perez explained. "They're rank-proud as sin."

Clanton looked at the dark-faced breed with new interest, the use of the little military phrase catching in his ear. "Where did you see service, Perez?"

"Scouted some fer General Price down in Texas."

"A scout for Price, eh? Well, you look skinny and dirty enough for a Confederate, at that. Now then, what about these Indians?"

Following Perez' instructions, the three white officers seated themselves opposite the visiting hostiles. There were no smiles now from the latter, no friendliness. Perez noted that Dull Knife and Two Moons both carried ceremonial pipes, that neither offered to light his. Dull Knife opened the talk.

"Today Makhpiya Luta made war on you. He had many warriors." Here the old chief held up his right hand, clenching it and flicking it open four or five times.

"Each flick is a hunderd," the scout asided to the officers, while Dull Knife orated on.

"He burned your train. He killed your soldiers. Red Cloud did this. He had American Horse with him. The Sioux did it."

Stacey's interrupting demand was suspicious. "Are you telling us the Cheyenne had no part in burning these wagons?"

"I am telling you that you cannot travel through the Sioux hunting grounds. It is the treaty. No white wagons will roll north of the Powder. The Eagle Chief has defied the treaty. He has gone against the tongue of the Grandfather. I, Dull Knife, tell you this."

"You are telling us?" Stacey took the role of spokesman for the three officers.

"No. I am telling you for Makhpiya Luta. He says you are going to build a great fort. That it is the plan to build this great fort, here, north of the Powder. Is this true? Is Red Cloud's tongue straight?"

"I can answer that question for you, Dull Knife," Clanton took over, having grabbed the tailgate of the conversation. "Red Cloud's tongue is straight. We are going to build such a fort."

There was silence then. For long minutes the only talk was between the quarreling coals of the dying fire. At last old Two Moons spoke.

"A fort will mean war. Makhpiya has said that. He has said, too, that you are going to build that fort. We thought he lied. Now we know he did not. Now there will be war. Makhpiya has said it. You can still go away. Go away, now. Ride your horses very fast. War is coming."

"When it comes, where will ye be, Uncle?" The question, soft as powder, came from Perez. Dull Knife answered for Two Moons.

"We shall be at peace if the Cut Throat People will let us. But you, Little Pony Stealer, should know how it is with them. You should know how it is with the Sioux. Maybe Makhpiya will not let us have peace."

"He won't," predicted the scout, flatly.

"Well, where are we now?" This, querulously, from Clanton. "As far as I can see you've told us nothing Red Cloud didn't tell us months ago down at Fort Loring."

"Yes, dammit," Stacey stepped in, quick-worded, his old impatience at work, "you heard Colonel Clanton tell Red Cloud and Crazy Horse we were going to come up here and build a fort. You talk with a big mouth, Dull Knife, but we

24

remember you. When Red Cloud and Crazy Horse got their asses up in the air and walked out on the peace talks, you walked with them. You were big for war then!" Stacy paused for breath, plunged recklessly on. "If you're through talking loud, get on your ponies and ride! We won't be bullied by a bunch of goddam, red—"

"Shet the fool up!" Perez' tight-lipped phrase went to Clanton, but the hard-faced Cheyenne were already on their feet.

"Yes, wait up, Stacey, I'll talk now." Addressing Dull Knife, the column commander spoke with his usual bluntness. "We know you are not threatening us and that your hearts are good."

The four chiefs hesitated, their narrowed eyes staring past the fire, not looking at any of the white officers. "But if the Sioux want war," Clanton's tones plodded implacably on, "they shall have it. And if the Cheyenne are with them, they shall have it, too."

Dull Knife took the long ceremonial pipe in its buckskin cover and slung it over his shoulder. His words were as dull as the glance of his old eyes. "We came to smoke the pipe with the Eagle Chief"—here his gaze flicked from Clanton to Stacey—"but the Oak Leaf Chief would not let us light it."

The Cheyenne were boarding their ponies. The talk was over. As usual, the white man had covered his ears.

Stacey, stung by the old chief's singling out of him as scapegoat for the conference's failure, sprang forward, seizing the hackamore of Dull Knife's pony. The old man's hand flashed to his shirt, came away with a bared knife. Before he could strike with it, a lean form shot under his pony's neck, driving a hunched shoulder into the officer's restraining arm, breaking its hold on the pony, sending its owner staggering backward.

"Ye goddam idjut!" Perez' exclamation lost none of its contempt for its quietness. "Don't ye know better'n to tech an Injun? Ye *never* lay hands onto an Injun!"

Stacey, shaken, livid with humiliation, rasped hoarsely, "You lousy goddam Sioux! If I had a gun I'd gut-shoot you where you stand. As it is"—the considerable attempt to regain control was partly successful—"this gallant display of concern for your red cousins will serve to get directly at what I had in mind asking the chief." With a quick nod to Colonel Clanton, he hurried on. "I was just going to ask the chief, here, to give us the thrilling account of your heroic defense of the wagon

25

train. Colonel Clanton seems inclined to credit your story so I thought it would be a shame to pass up this chance to interview four undoubted eyewitnesses. Their testimony will surely tend to clear you, Perez."

Clanton, entirely missing the irony of his second's speech, at once agreed. "Of course. Good idea, Stacey. Perhaps these savages can help you at that, Perez. I hadn't thought of it."

"I had," said Perez, flatly, twisting his thin mouth with the words.

"Well, go ahead then, man," the officer instructed the scout, "ask them about the fight. I'd like to hear what they have to say, and I'd like to hear them clear you if they can."

"No." The half-breed's refusal was surprisingly blunt. "Git yer own information out'n them. Thet way mebbeso ye'll believe it."

"All right, Stacey," Clanton nodded, shortly, "go ahead."

The major, with a forced bow to Perez, turned upon Dull Knife with patent pleasure. "The Eagle Chief wants to know about this great fighter, here," jerking a disdainful thumb at Perez, "this Little Pony Stealer, how he defended the wagon train, how he fought till the last white was slain, how he slew the Sioux by the hundreds, how he—"

The old Cheyenne looked at the truculent officer, contempt as plainly painted on his features as the vermilion and ocher designs which otherwise daubed them. "The Oak Leaf Chief thinks to make a fool of the Cheyenne. He thinks to make Dull Knife appear like a little boy. And to make Pony Stealer a killer of the white brother. Now we shall see." The old man's phrases dropped with precise devastation into the breath-held silence. It was still enough to hear the flicking of a pony's ear. "We were not at the fight." Dull Knife stared over Stacey's head, looking at the man, not looking at him. "I, myself, did not see it. But Makhpiya Luta has placed a price of fifty ponies for the scalp of Little Pony Stealer, and American Horse, himself, has sworn he will get those fifty ponies. Let that tell you how your prisoner fought this day."

There was a slit-eyed pause during which Dull Knife shifted his stare to Clanton. "I respect the Eagle Chief," he said at last, "so let him hear this. The scouts have flashed the glass from the south. Makhpiya Luta knows about your Pony Soldiers. They are small and they are lost. A single, One-Bar Chief leads them. A young, white squaw follows. They are all lost."

He and the other chiefs wheeled their ponies toward Perez.

"H'g'un!" The deep voice of the Cheyenne War Chief went to the scout, rolling out the Sioux word for courage, a lifted, right-arm salute accompanying it.

"H'g'un! H'g'un! H'g'un!" echoed his followers, each in turn saluting.

"Woyuonihan," responded the scout, his face as expressionless as theirs. Then, as they turned their ponies' rumps to the fire, he called out after them, *"Mani Wakan Tanka!"* The Cheyenne acknowledged this prayer for them to walk in the shadow of the Great Spirit's protection, with backward handwaves. The darkness reached out and swallowed them almost before the white officers realized they were moving to go.

Clanton stared after them a moment, turned abruptly on Stacey, blue eyes for once snapping with decision.

"Cut Perez loose, Stacey. You can count him under technical arrest if you will, but I think fifty ponies is price enough to at least take the ropes off a man." With the scowling major stepping toward the prisoner, the column commander concluded, "And get your thirty men mounted up, Stacey. You're going down the trail, tonight." For a space, then, they all waited as Clanton enjoyed his little moment. Almost, you could hear him smacking his lips over it. His words, when they came, spun Stacey around in disbelief, brought Perez to his feet, eyes shining with fierce hope. "Don't worry about losing your way, Major. You'll have the best guide on the Virginia City Road out in front of you."

2 MAKHPIYA LUTA

The War Chief

THE NIGHT WAS RINGING-CLEAR AS A TEMPLE BELL. THE FAT
September stars were a wild-scattered giant's firebed of white-
blinking coals, windspread across the black hearth of the
Wyoming skies. Their clustering myriads swarmed low over
the hulking shoulders of the Wolf Mountains to the north,
swam in firefly millions among the shining peaks of the Big
Horns to the west. Under their light the Virginia City Road
lay dust-still, its dim track stretching away southward, sixty
miles to Fort Keene.

On a ridge above the trail, To-Ke-Ya, the dog fox, left off
his business of mouse hunting to flick his nervous ears northward up the starlit Road. For a moment he remained motionless, one daintily reaching forefoot held in mid-air, sharp,
black face backing the flat, yellow eyes as they stared, un-
blinking in the direction from whence the disturbance came.

Presently the shifting, furry cones isolated the foreign vibra-
tions. For another moment, then, To-Ke-Ya froze, big ears
working the evening breeze. Quickly the warning sound
swelled, grew presently into a staccato rhythm even a dull
human ear could not fail to catalogue—the drum-fire roll of
hoofbeats galloping in the night.

To-Ke-Ya watched the pony of the loose-swinging rider
pound past his hiding place and disappear down the gloomy
Road. For a moment he wondered, idly, what the little yellow
sunke wakan and his Indian rider had been in such a hurry

about. Then he growled in dismissal of the whole subject, trotting over to urinate disdainfully on a handy elder bush. What did he care about a lone Sioux rider pounding down the trail? Or about the young Army lieutenant and the beautiful white girl lost in the hills of the Road thirty miles below? Or about that other group of figures moving in the night ten miles to the east? The group going at a jingling trot? That group whose unshod ponies shuffled by the hundreds through the silent dust. Whose naked, red riders went slit-eyed through the night, feathered war-bonnets and tasseled lances bobbing and glinting in the starlight.

No, the dog fox had no time for half-breed wagon guides, or green lieutenants, or young white squaws, or Sioux War Chiefs. Not tonight. Not just now. To-Ke-Ya had a mouse to catch!

It was 2 A.M. when Perez slowed the rattailed dun out of his hours-long gallop. The little gelding was beginning to run rough, letting the scout know he had no more than ten miles left in him. He had carried Perez thirty miles from Clanton's camp, twenty past To-Ke-Ya's ridge. Ahead, now, a black ribbon athwart the trail, lay Squaw Creek.

Coming down the long decline of Connor's Ridge, the scout walked, hand-leading the gelding, letting him blow out along the rock-strewn downgrade. At the ford he led him out into the shallow stream, letting him drink a little before tying his muzzle up so that he could take no more. Then he scooped handfuls of dripping moss and mountain cress from the stream's floor, sponging these over the little dun's laboring flanks. The cool creek water quieted the horse and shortly Perez led him away, putting him to graze in a patch of hay along the stream. The scout watched the gelding closely, then, seeing him begin to eat, nodded to himself. Good. A man could see the horse would make it. Waste. *H'g'un.* He'd hate to have broke the little devil's wind just getting away from those club-headed soldiers. "*H'g'un*, Sosi," he called softly to him in Sioux, "yer heart's as big as a buffalo's bottom."

The little gelding left off his grazing to look up. Sosi was quite a horse and he knew it. Despite a score of arrow and lance scars, one eye gone to a Pied Noir knife thrust and half his teeth knocked out by a Kangi Wicasi stone ax, he could outgo any pony on the plains. Now, looking at his master, he decided flattery wasn't going to get the dark breed anywhere. Soft words didn't make up for hard riding. With a flirt of his rump and an arrogant, nose-clearing snort, Sosi returned to his grazing.

Perez grinned, knocked out the pipe he had lit, ground the coals with a twist of his moccasin. It was time to ride. A man didn't have to look twice at the shift of those stars to know that dawn wasn't two hours off.

Briefly, the scout calculated his position. Two things he knew, two he assumed. He knew Clanton had broken camp, was night marching on the double down the Virginia City Road. He knew Stacey was out in front of Clanton with the thirty mounted infantry. He assumed Lieutenant Collins and the Colonel's daughter were somewhere on his, Perez', front, lost in the hills flanking the trail. He assumed Red Cloud was somewhere in the hills, too, but definitely not lost.

Perez, though freed of his bonds, had still been under technical arrest when, hours before, he had deserted Stacey's column. To Perez the desertion was logical: he had made a smart plan and bluffed the *Wasicun* commander into falling for it. Now he was free by virtue of his own brainwork. By the same token, he was damned if he wasn't going to stay that way. He had done nothing. A man would be worse than feeble-minded to let them punish him for something he hadn't done. A man sets himself enough traps to step into along the trail-line of his life, without he's got to go stepping into snares laid for him by others. The hell with it. He was loose and by God he was aiming to stay that way.

To Stacey, the desertion was treacherous, wholly vindicatory of his original suspicion and opinion of the breed. Furious with Clanton for having technically freed the half-Indian guide on the testimony of the Cheyenne chiefs, furious with himself for letting the hated half-breed outwit him and slip away, 2:30 A.M. found Major Phil Stacey blundering down the Bozeman two hours north of Squaw Creek.

Two-thirty A.M. found other things. It found the smoke of Lieutenant Wilke Collins' banked campfires curling thin and white up out of the hilled-in meadow where he and his forty troopers slumbered peacefully, slumbered with their rifles stacked, their horses grazing far off-picket. Once it had climbed up past the sheltering hilltops, that thin, white smoke lay hard and clear against the prairie skies, visible for miles in every direction. Letters of fire as tall as ten warriors couldn't have advertised Lieutenant Collins' position any better. To eyes schooled in the ways of the High Plains, that thin, white smoke clearly spelled: "Quiet, Please. Many Foolish Men Sleeping. Approach without Caution. Slaughter at Will."

Perez saw that smoke ten minutes after he remounted and left Squaw Creek. Curses flew then with an evil fluency never learned in the war camps. That had to be Lieutentant Collins. Who but a green Army man would leave night fires smoking in the gut of hostile Indian country?

Perez shrugged. It was nothing to him. He was well out of the whole mess. Let the fools die. He started on, cursed, pulled Sosi up hard again.

How about the girl, Perez? How about her, Pawnee? Your friend the colonel's daughter? The one Stacey had said was the most beautiful girl in the world? What about her? Let her die, too? Did you owe the colonel anything? Like maybe the fact you were free right now? How about that? How about the Eagle Chief? Was it Courtesy Rules between you and him? Respect, Pawnee? And honor? *Woyuonihan! Wowicake!* So it was true. Did an Indian, then, pay his debts? Did a foster-son of the Oglala Bad Faces, a dedicated war-child of the Cheyenne Cut Arms, show the heels of his honor to the *Wasicun?* Did the son of a Pawnee chief's daughter forget his manners? *Aii-eeel Waugh!* Did the rain fall down and the grass grow up?

Sosi grunted in pained surprise as the moccasined heels pistoned into his ribs. Flattening his belly to the ground, the mud-colored gelding went up and over the low hillside to the left of the trail, his hoofs scrambling and clawing like a scared cat's. On the other side Sosi found a narrow, level gully, running easterly, toward the smokes. Perez pointed the gelding down this tortuous track, giving him his head. "Go on, ye crap-colored cut-stud," he whispered savagely in the little horses' pinned-back ear, "run yer rotten yaller heart out!"

Sosi ran then and he ran fast. But ten miles to the east other ponies were running, and they were running fast, too. The eyes of Makhpiya Luta were as bright and black as those of Pawnee Perez. He had seen that smoke even better than the half-breed. After all, the War Chief had been three miles closer to it when he saw it.

Within a mile of the smoke, Perez brought the gelding into a walk. He had seen nothing, heard less. But that sky-crawling smoke was such an inviting signature of helplessness that he knew if the Sioux were within ten miles of it they would be riding it down like squaws after a crippled calf. A man could look to his hair along about here. Chances were, those hills ahead were as full of Oglala lances as they were of sword-grass spikes. The half-breed had the gelding walking, and walking very softly. It was as well he did.

While the runty dun picked his way through the cow's belly black of the gully, his rider kept his glance fastened on the best signpost available. In the trace of starlight filtering down to the gulch bottom, Perez could just make out the little beast's bobbing head, and not for an instant did he take his eyes away from those flicking ears. Back and forth they moved, those ears, in regular cadence with Sosi's tossing forelock. Forward and back. Forward and back. Forward—and then, suddenly—staying forward, sharp-pricked.

Perez stiffened, leaning along the gelding's wiry neck, right arm reaching up along the jug head, hand clawed, tense, ready. In a moment Sosi's head swung up, following the point of his ears. He flared his nostrils, sucking in the cold air blowing fresh from the east. As his mount got his nose full of the wind, the scout sensed the stiffening that raced down his back. Instantly the poised hand dove for Sosi's nose, clamping it hard. Another second and Perez was off him and had a wrap of the hackamore rope around his muzzle. Then he stood with him, both man and horse straining their senses out through the darkness.

Perez' nose wasn't as good as Sosi's but it wasn't much less so. Softly, the scout blew out through his nostrils, clearing them two or three times. Then his head swung back and forth across the breeze. Not thirty seconds after the gelding's ears first shot forward, Perez had the scent himself. It was pungent, acrid, stinking, and to the scout it smelled of one smell—many ponies, close-packed, warm with traveling.

No forty-odd, cooled-out cavalry mounts were going to put that potent a flavor into the night air, by God. It was a gut-cinch he'd been right about looking to his hair. Perez felt the short bristles at the nape of his neck lift.

Somewhere ahead of him, between where he stood and Lieutenant Collins' campfires, were several hundred Indian ponies. And unless Perez missed his reckoning, each one of them was carrying a rider of other hue than white. When a man was born in a skin lodge, weaned on a rawhide cradle-board, cut his teeth on an eagle-bone whistle, and grew up with the delicate stench of woodsmoke, boiled dog, tanned hides and horse dung constantly in his nostrils, he got so he could "smell Indian."

Perez was "smelling Indian" now. Lots of it. Very close.

He couldn't have more than minutes left to do whatever he was going to do. Dawn came early in this northern country. With the first streaks of it, the Oglala would go pouring down on that cavalry camp from every gully flanking it. Perez reckoned the time to be somewhere after three-thirty. On a night as clear as this, faint gray would come right hard after four.

The scout right off discarded the idea of going around the Indians. If a man was going to get into that sleeping camp, there, ahead of Oglala, by God he'd just have to wade through them.

Keeping his tight wrap on the gelding's nose, Perez led him forward through the dark, his eyes straining over the dimness of the gully floor. Shortly, he saw it: a dense clump of poplar scrub. Urging the dun into this cover, he snubbed him up tight to a four-inch sapling, cinched the nose-wrap down with cruel hardness. You didn't play with kindness in this company. That was for sure as hell.

Unbuckling both Colts, he wrapped them in their belts, hid them under a tangle of dry twigs. The Winchester followed suit. Next, the fringed buckskin leggins and hunting shirt.

When Perez came out of that poplar clump, he came out naked save for three things: the chamois-soft moccasins on his feet, the deerskin crotch-cloth about his loins, the lean Spanish knife in his right hand.

You didn't see him go up the ridge out of the gully. One minute he was standing outside the clump; the next, he appeared along the top of the ridge—not the top, either, but just below the top. And that is where he went along, just below the top, crouching and swift as a hunting painter. Perez knew well enough to stay off any skyline, no matter it looked plumb dark. A man could think a night is black but he by God better remember that no night is as black as the sudden hulking up of a body atop any elevation backed by sky.

As the half-breed went slinking along the shoulder of the ridge, that feeling began to get into him. *Ai-eee!* Just when a man got to figuring he'd got rid of it, it came back on him. Seemed like every time it would come to him was when he would get to cat-and-mousing it around with Yunke-lo.

Yunke-lo was the Sioux Shade of Death, and once the old black bastard got into the game, Perez never felt quite like the *Wasicun* wagon guide he wanted so hard to be.

There was something about the clean feel of the wind on

the nakedness of a man's body. In the feel of the hard muscles running taut and springy through every inch of you. To the firm, sure feel of the friendly ground under your stalking moccasins. To the power-feel of the knife haft in your hand, with its beautiful balance of blade thrilling a man as though he held something alive. There was that very smell that got in your nostrils when the hunt tightened up like this. Perez never really knew what it was, this smell, but it shrank the membranes of the nose, flaring the passages and making them feel stinging clean. Sometimes it made a man think, almost, that it was the body-stink of old man Yunke-lo himself. Sometimes, times like just now, a man got to wondering, even as Perez was wondering now, if he didn't know how death smelled.

And more. If, knowing the smell, a man didn't get to liking it?

These were the times Pawnee Perez knew his blood. These were the times that made a man know his color, his heart, the wildness that was red line-bred into him, that was always there, just beneath the thin, pale veneer of the *Wasicun*. That instinct to hunt, stalk, trap, to destroy, that ran so close beneath the hard, white shell he'd built up so carefully around himself. These were the times Perez knew what he was. And what he knew was that the Oglala beyond that ridge weren't the only Indians abroad that frosty morning.

After paralleling the ridge for about three hundred yards, the scout topped it. The stink of men and horses was now so thick it hit a man in the face like a heavy-swung, sour blanket. Belly-flat, Perez hugged the spine of the ridge, peering silently downward.

Spread before him was a cuplike little valley, half a mile in diameter. Out in the flat of the opening, closer to the other side, loomed the white cluster of the Army tents. Over against the far side of the valley, a clump of heavy tree growth butted up against perpendicular, low cliffs. Another clump choked the ravine in front of and below his position. Otherwise, except for the waist-high summer hay which filled the valley, the ground was open and clear all around the campsite.

By the faint sights and sounds which came up to him from the grove below, the jingle of metal harness, the dust-deadened stamping of ponies' hoofs, the occasional flash of a white feather headdress, or dull glint of a gun barrel or lance blade in the starlight, Perez knew the growth crawled with Indians. After a few seconds he began to believe the whole group of

Oglala was down there. The sign that kept coming up to him spelled hundreds. Apparently Red Cloud was so sure of this camp he hadn't circled it. It semed the Oglala leader had kept his command intact, probably planning one big frontal rush as soon as there was a streak of light to run by.

Perez showed his white teeth. The quick grimace could pass for a grin only by the rarest stretch of charity. It pleased the scout, professionally, to know that even the great Makhpiya Luta got careless. It pleased him even more that Wakan Tanka, the Great Spirit, had given it to Perez, the half-breed Pawnee, to show the vaunted War Chief the hole in his warbonnet. If, indeed, the Oglala *had* neglected to fill that other grove across the valley with warriors. Counting he hadn't, by God, a man could still put a stiff crimp in his Sioux tail. Of course, if the grove over beyond the sleeping camp *was* loaded with slit-eyes, the half-breed's little plan wouldn't be worth a cottontail's chance in a bush full of beagles. But if the grove proved empty, well, time enough to worry about crowing after he found out it wasn't. Meantime there was a hazard or two between the scout and his first goal: reaching those tents ahead of, and unknown to, Red Cloud. Yes, a hazard or two.

Like, say, for instance, those four hundred Oglala down there.

Silently, Perez cursed the shortness of time. Given twenty minutes he could have circled the little valley, coming into the soldier camp from the far side. As it was, he had to go straight in from where he lay—straight in and wading armpit-deep through a bunch of trigger-nerved hostiles.

Withal, he wasn't on the ridge three minutes before he went gliding down its far side and into the hidden hundreds below. His medicine was good. Sometimes a man mixed it up in a hurry and it came out that way, Scores of other figures as naked and red as his own were crouching or moving about in the cover.

At first he went forward rapidly. Once he bumped squarely into a sneaking brave, as the two of them rounded the same tree.

"*Wonunicun,*" grunted Perez. "It was a mistake."

"Who is it?" whispered the other.

"High-Back-Bear," Perez responded, using the name of a minor chief he knew to be along. "And keep your flapping mouth closed. You jabber like a squaw. Makhpiya will cut your wobbling tongue out!"

"*Ai-eee!* Even so. Good hunting, brother."

"Be still," growled Perez, and turned quickly away.

When almost free of the woods, his reaching foot landed soundly in squirming flesh.

"By Pte's navell!" came the hoarse rasp from the ground. "If you must go strolling at such a time, keep your big foot out of my mouth."

"*Wonunicun,*" apologized Perez.

"Who is it?" The challenge came swiftly.

"High-Back-Bear."

"Oh. Well, many *coups,* cousin."

"Shhh!" admonished the half-breed, going quickly forward.

Another moment and he felt the waist-high grass of the valley around him and he knew he was out of the woods. With a long sigh, he dropped to his belly, began snaking out toward the cavalry camp. He had gone ten yards when his outstretched hand closed over a human leg. He felt the flesh contract, then the guttural voice was grunting. "Who it is, there? Who touched me?"

"*Kola, tahunsa,*" muttered Perez, "a friend, cousin. Is this the last line out?"

"Aye. Forty of us, with American Horse. One every three pony lengths. We lead the attack."

"I can scarcely wait for the first light," probed Perez.

"Aye, the first light. That is when we go. Be patient, brother."

"I come from Makhpiya," the half-breed whispered, letting his voice grow stern. "He wants me to go up a little way more. *Mani Wakan Tanka,* brother. May your arrows not wobble."

Slithering past the other, Perez felt the hand reach for him and lock like a vice on his left arm. The deep voice purred with suspicion. "Who did you say you were, cousin?"

"Shut up, you *heyoka!* You want to wake all the Pony Soldiers? I didn't say."

"You are saying now. I don't like the sound of your voice. Too soft. Who is it?"

"High-Back-Bear!" As Perez uttered the name he heard the sibilant intake of the other's breath. Instantly the scout knew the masquerade was over. His right arm whipped backward and up, flashing the thin Spanish knife into split-poised readiness.

"A small world, brother." The unseen enemy's heavy voice was bare audible. "I, too, am High-Back-Bear!" With the

Oglala's words Perez felt the hand on his left arm tighten spasmodically, knew what it meant. Had it been broad daylight he couldn't have seen the knife coming more clearly.

He rolled into the Indian, feeling the other's striking arm thud across his bare back, feeling the knife miss, feeling its vicious blade graze the skin of his far side. At the same time he hurled his own blade down and forward, whipping it straight in. He heard the sodden, ripe-pumpkin "tunk!" as the knife went home, felt the hot blood gush over his hand and wrist. An instant later the grip of the hand on his left wrist slackened, fell open, then flaccidly away.

"H'g'un!" whispered Perez, twisting his blade free. "It's a bad night for high-backed-bears."

Ten minutes later he lay alongside the tent of Second Lieutenant Wilke Collins, listening to the breathing of its occupants. That was a little strange, by damn. He hadn't thought to find anyone sharing the lieutenant's tent. Must be another officer along, after all. Commissioned men weren't in the habit of tent-sharing with troopers. Sliding around to the front of the tent, Perez parted the flap and eased in.

Behind him the first thin tinge of gray picked out the gleaming peaks of the Big Horns.

Crawling into that tent was like wriggling into the unopened gut of a grizzly—it was that black. But it wasn't the blackness that caused Perez to freeze just inside the flap. It was the smell!

Ai-eee, that smell had no right to be in an Army tent two hundred miles north of the last civilized post on the frontier. It was a smell that made every nerve fiber in a man's body pull up tight as a strung bow. It was purely delicious, that smell. A smell that any man of Perez' ferine nature would recognize instantly. As instantly as the prowling wolf would know the bitch, or the pirating wild stud the mare.

There was a woman in that tent.

Perez trembled, sudden perspiration breaking over him like a warm breath. His stomach drew inward on itself till it felt like a clenched ball no bigger than his knotted fist. The great muscles of his back tensed aching-tight down the long arch of his spine. His chest felt compressed, his throat constricted, his nostrils pinched. A moment before, a naked red Indian had slipped through that tent flap. Now, in his place, crouched a confused and trembling white wagon guide.

Perez knew the sensation which gripped him was a new one. The mood which had seized him when he started in through the Oglala was gone, leaving this strange, nerve-tingling unrest, this deep, good-feeling thing he had never known before. He went forward into the tent, high-strung as a panther on sucking-colt tracks. If the Pawnees had a Cupid, he had just shot Pawnee Perez square through the crotch-cloth.

It was no trick to find the man. It was easy to smell a man out in the dark. First, you had just the male-smell, which was good enough for any stalker worth the name, but then you usually had the cloying fragrance of tobacco, too. And in this case, the scout noted, there was another designator present, not at all unfamiliar to the frontier nor to Perez: trade whiskey fumes.

What a breakfast dish to be setting before the hawk-bridged noses of four hundred hostile Sioux! A sleeping camp of forty green men and a lone white woman, in charge of a raw junior lieutenant heavily at work snoring off a big drunk!

As soon as he smelled the whiskey, Perez was afraid to touch the man. Wakan Tanka knew it was nervy enough awakening any soldier sleeping in Indian country. To arouse a green officer out of a liquor stupor could be suicide.

Still, there was no time to go prowling the camp looking for the sergeants. He had to find them, sure, and Gold help a man if they weren't as seasoned as Clanton had said, but he couldn't just crawl around blind among all those tents, scratching and whispering for Murphy and Moriarity.

It had to be the woman, then. He had to find out from her where they were. God could kiss them all good-by if she made an outcry, too.

Even as he went toward her, Perez wondered at the odd morals of the whites—a colonel's daughter sleeping in the same tent with a strange lieutenant. True, they were bedded separate, but—

"Ma'am!" whispered Perez, "wake up, ma'am!" His reaching hand touched bare flesh, warmer and softer than spring wind. He felt rather than heard the indrawn, stiffening gasp from the woman, brought his hand away as though from a hot stove lid. "Ma'am, for God's sake don't make no noise. If ye do, we're all daid. Don't talk, jest listen." He could see the whites of her eyes, now, staring wide at his bulking shadow, could feel the quick sweet breath of her on his bare arm.

"Who are you?" she whispered. "Quick, or I'll cry out!"

Perez knew there was great fear in the voice, knew the whole thing hung in the balance of his next words. "John Perez. Government scout with Colonel Clanton." The half-breed wing-shot the flying lie out of the naked air, hoping it would sound right. "Are ye Miss Lura?"

"Yes, I'm Lura Clanton." Her voice was controlled, steady, letting Perez know his gamble had succeeded.

"Yer father sent me," the scout lied, "Listen to me and make your answers fast and straight. Thar's over four hundred hostile Sioux in them hills west of hyar. They'll attack this camp in about fifteen minutes. Do ye understand thet?"

Her answer was a stifled gasp, then the quiet words, "Yes, I understand. Go on."

Perez nodded to himself. A man could tell this white squaw was no *heyoka*. She would do to ride the river with. "Listen, the lieutenant is drunk, ain't he?"

"Yes."

"All right. I want the sergeants. Murphy and Moriarity. Whar are they?"

"The next tent, I think. I'm not sure."

"I'm goin'," Perez warned. "Now, listen. Ye're a white woman. Ye sleep in a tent with a strange man so I know ye're a full woman, too. Ye got thet?"

"I don't know what you mean! Why, I—"

"Shet up. I'll be back fer ye. While I'm gone I want ye should git the lieutenant awake. Ye know whut I mean. Wake him up like a woman. Git over thar under thet blanket with him. Thet'll bring the blood, flush his mind out, mebbe. Keep him from yellin' out, anyways. Thar's no time fer anythin' else."

"I—I don't know I—"

"Goddam ye, don't ask me whut I mean, *Wasicun*. I felt ye and I kin smell ye. Ye're all woman. Git over thar and wake thet drunk son of a bitch up. And wake him up gentle!" Perez went out of the tent in a running crouch, not waiting to see what Lura Clanton did.

Slipping into the next tent, he called out, voice low but no longer whispering. "Murphy? Moriarity? Ye sergeants in hyar. Wake up. Whar are ye?"

"We're awake enough, laddie buck. Another step without yez had called out, and yez'd bin asleep, though. Ease off wid yer carbine, now, Danny me bye. Let's see whut this little man is wantin'. Whut'll yez be after dyin' to know, laddie? And by the bye, do yez mind tellin' us who yez are?"

39

"I'm John Perez, regular scout with Colonel Clanton," he repeated the lie. "We run into Red Cloud up north. He's out in force. Wouldn't tackle Clanton's column but he found out about yer outfit—" The half-breed broke off, abruptly. "Are ye other men awake? Listenin'?"

"Yeah."

"Shore."

"What in Ned's the matter?"

"The matter," Perez' voice raced, now, "is thet Red Cloud is out thar in them west hills. Thar's better'n four hundred Oglala Bad Faces with him, and the whole passel of 'em's goin' to be down on the camp in about eight minutes."

"Lord, Gawd A'mighty—"

The half-breed's growling voice interrupted. "If ye're hankerin' to keep yer hair, shet up and listen. Thar's no chancet to save nothin'. No horses, no food, nothin'. Ye got thet? Happen ye git out'n this camp with yer rifle and enough head-fuzz to keep yer skull settled, ye're luckier then a two-foot dog to tie a four-foot bitch. East of hyar, two hundred yards, thar's a big alder clump up agin some low cliffs. Do ye mark the spot, Murphy?" Perez picked the first sergeant for his query, liking the way he'd talked up when he'd sneaked into the tent. Murphy's short answer let him know he'd picked right.

"Yes sir, I do."

"Good. The bunch of ye in this tent git out and wake up every man in camp. No lights, no loud talkin'. And hurry, soft. Them Injuns kin hear a field mouse bark further than ye kin a mule bray."

"All right, byes. Ye hear thet, now?" Murphy's voice cut in, low and quick. "Whut else, Mister Perez?"

"When ye've got them awake, start them movin' fer thet alder clump—on their bellies! Each man takes his carbine and all the ammunition he kin tote. Thar'll be no orders and don't wait fer none. Jest hit fer that clump. Any noise and the Sioux'll be up yer butt a yard and a half afore ye kin cinch yer puckerin' strings. Ye got the smell of thet, clean?"

"Yes, sir," Murphy again, speaking for the rest. "Whut kind of a chance have we got?"

"If we kin make thet clump without Red Cloud knows it, we got a good chancet. Major Stacey is jest two hours back of me, with thirty horses. Close enough to easy hear the firin' when it starts. He'll come on in, fast, when he does. Colonel Clanton is comin' up behind him with the whole column." The scout made it sound as good as he could. "All depends on how long we kin hold the Sioux once the lead starts to gittin' slang. Happen we kin stand them off till noon, we'll make it. But thet's six, seven hours," the purring voice dropped flat. "Right now we got mebbe five, ten minutes. Let's go. And let's go fast. I'll git Lieutenant Collins and the girl."

The drunken lieutenant may have been grass-green, but Sergeant Murdo Murphy was that color by nativity only. "All right, yez hairy-assed apes. Yez heard Mister Perez. Git goin'! And the first one of yez whut so much as breaks wind is goin' to git his barkin' buttside knocked off by me, Murphy, personal. Danny, yez wake up the south half of the tents, I'll git the north."

Sergeant Danny Moriarity, Murphy's opposite number, was a cheerful man. His response sat good with Perez, making the half-breed know that Clanton hadn't overfigured either non-com. "Jest as yez say, Murdo, me bye. Soft and easy."

The tent was cleared in seconds. Perez, running, low-bent, back toward Collins' tent, could see some of the men, shadow-silent, already snaking out into the tall grass, heading for the alder grove. Good, by God! This thing might yet work out a mite slanchwise from the way Makhpiya Luta had it figured.

"Ready, ma'am?" his low voice went in at the tent flap. His answer came from the looming figure of Lieutenant Wilke Collins.

"Who're you? What the hell's going on around here? By God, I'll—" The voice was loud, blatant, thick with whiskey. There was a trace of light, now, allowing Perez to see the weaving bulk of the officer's body—and Collins to see the half-breed.

Perez saw the lieutenant's face drain white as he realized he was looking at a naked, red Sioux, knew the next instant would bring the drunken officer's alarm yell of "Indians!"

The half-breed shot through the tent flap, circling and coming up fast, his left arm seeking and finding the lieutenant's neck from the rear. Throwing his knee up hard into the man's kidneys, Perez bent him far back over his braced thigh.

"Thet's a knife in yer ribs, friend." His white teeth chopped at the words. "If ye make one more noise, ye'll git it all the way into yer liver." Collins stopped struggling, breathing hard, rolling the whites of his eyes up through the tent-gloom. "Ye're slobberin' drunk, but try and git this through yer pickled skull. This camp is goin' to be under Sioux attack in about four minutes. I've ordered all yer men out and I've come back fer ye

41

and the girl. We're goin' to try fer them trees agin the east bluff. Either ye're comin' with us or ye're stayin' hyar. Whut do ye say?" Here, easing the clamping forearm away from the throat, the scout tacked a little rider onto the tail of his proposition. "If ye stay hyar, it'll be with this knife splittin' yer ribs. I don't aim to have no slopped-up shavetail left behind me when I move outa hyar. Leastways, not one in no condition to be makin' any noise. Understand?"

"Yes, yes! Let's go. No, wait a minute. Who the hell do you think you are to be ordering me around? Where're we going? Where's Lura? Goddammit, I'll not be—" His voice started to rise again and Perez stepped back and struck him, palm-flat, across the face.

"Get out!" The scout shoved the stumbling officer through the tent flap, tripping him on his face as he went out. "And git down on yer damn belly and stay thar!"

Turning to the girl, he touched her shoulder, all the old softness back in his voice. "Come on, ma'am. Down on your hands and knees. Right out through this tall grass, hyar."

The girl, who had been watching him, as fascinated as a child staring at a tiger, obeyed without a murmur.

"Crawl straight fer those cliffs ahaid, ma'am. The lieutenant'll foller you with me right behind him so's to see he don't git lost. Hurry up, ma'am. We're the last ones out." The girl slid ahead as instructed, Lieutenant Collins, cursing and muttering in slack-jawed confusion, crawling after her.

Before following them in, Perez took a last look and listen, west. The dawn-streak had slid from the east, clear around the prairie, backing the distant Big Horns with a luminous gray, though the low hills surrounding the little valley still crouched in darkness. Even as Perez watched, the gray broke out from behind the far peaks, tipping the near hills with silver. A fox barked querulously in the grass near the west grove. Another answered him from within the grove. A poorwill whipped sleepily farther along the hills. Its mate called dolorously back. Perez couldn't resist the temptation.

To the straining ears of the Oglala, nerve-keyed for the go-word from the War Chief, an eerie howl came drifting from beyond the dark soldier camp—long, low, incredibly sad, the hunting song of the buffalo wolf, tribal danger-call of the South Plains Pawnee.

Hearing it, Makhpiya Luta straightened. Under him, his pinto stud, hearing it, too, pinned his ears and walled his eyes. For a moment the War Chief hesitated.

"It is nothing." Elk Nation spoke from the shadows to Red Cloud's left. "Truly a *sunke manitu*, a wolf, nothing more."

"Aye," agreed Buffalo Runner, looming up on the War Chief's left, "no Pawnees around here. Just a wolf. *Hopo*, let's go."

"No doubt you are right," growled the Oglala leader, uneasily. "But for a moment, there, I thought—"

"*Hookahey*. Come on. Let's go," urged Elk Nation. "This is the time."

"All right. Our hearts are brave, not afraid of wolves— or Pawnee spirits. Here we go." Red Cloud tightened his knees on the pinto stud, threw back his head, rolled his deep war-cry down the waiting line. "*Hiii-yeee-hahhh! Hopo*, let's go!"

"*Hookahey! Hookahey! Hookahey!*" echoed snarlingly from the four hundred throats before all human sound was drowned in the hammer of the ponies' hoofs.

To look at Lura Clanton you would miss her just as far as young Wilke Collins had when he'd met her in St. Louis the month before—or as Pawnee Perez had when he'd whispered to her in the blackened tent.

To see her you would say, first, that she was beautiful. And you would be as right as sun in August. Beauty sparkled in every clear feature of her face, every feline curve of her body. She was a flashing red-blonde, tall, fair, fascinatingly handsome, full-formed, strong, graceful and quick as a cat.

Then, secondly, you would say she was wicked. And you would be wrong. As surely wrong as the difference between wickedness and wildness.

To actually know her you would say something else. Maybe something like what Sergeant Murdo Murphy was saying to Perez as the two lay in the east grove waiting for Red Cloud to charge the deserted camp.

"Jest between I and yerself, now, Perez, I don't know as they was ever married. Lieutenant Collins brung her along when he reported in at Fort Lorin' two weeks ago. Story goes they was married in St. Louie, but I don't know. Fer all she's the Old Man's daughter, she's a wild one. Wild eyes and wild ways. Looks at a man in a way thet'll set him on fire, whether she wants him burnin' or not.

"When Lieutenant Collins first got to the fort yez could see right away he was a boozer, but mind yez, nothin' like he got to be.

43

"At first the two of them acted fairly decent. Then he begun drinkin' heavy and's bin drunk as Flannagan's goat ever since. If yez ask me, thet redheaded blonde girl is the cause of all this trouble. Seems she run away from the convent in St. Louie, took up with the lieutenant, come west with him to the fort, telegraphed her old man she was comin' on up to Fort Keene with Collins. Of course the Old Man telegraphed back to Colonel Boynton, he's the C.O. at Fort Lorin', to hold her down there. Yez kin see whut good it done. Why, she had the colonel wropped around her little pinky in three days, and him fresh from buryin' his lovin' wife not these two months gone. Like I was sayin', Perez, if yez ask me—"

"Wal, I didn't ask ye fer no old lady's latrine report on whut she does with what God stuck under her petticoat, Sergeant. And I don't hold it agin a flossie none if she's got a waggle to her seat. Suits me fine to see somethin' shimmyin' back of a female when she waltzes herse'f around. All I asked ye was whether or not Lieutenant Collins was very drunk last night."

"Last night and every night since we left the fort. They was trouble between him and the gurl. They kept to the tent together but was sleepin' separate."

"I know thet, too," Perez said quickly. "But all I wanted to learn was if ye thought Collins was too drunk to fight his command. When I took over back there in the camp and right now, I mean."

"Absolutely."

"Thet's your opinion beyond changin'?"

"Yes, sir."

"Wal, ye jest remember it, Sergeant, because I'm takin' over official, as of right now. I mean I'm takin' Collins' command. Ye understand? Ye know whut the Army thinks about havin' its commissions kicked around and ye know whut insubordination is."

"Yes, sir."

"It's safer to pull a suckin' cub off a sore-tit sow grizzly then to steal a command thisaway. Ye're liable to get yer ass busted clear back to a buck fer takin' orders from me and ignorin' Collins."

"Yes, sir."

"Wal, whut do ye say? Will ye take them?"

"I'll not only take them, Perez, I'll see that every wet-eared scut in the company takes 'em."

"All right, now, listen. Ye take half the men, Moriarity

44

the other half. Lay them out along the front of the woods, yers to my right, Moriarity's to my left. No firin' till I give the word. And pay no attention to Lieutenant Collins, no matter whut."

"Yes, sir."

"Git goin'. The light's on the hills. We'll hear from our friends across the way any minute."

As if in answer to Perez' prediction, a long-drawn *"Hiii-yeee-haaa!"* broke the quiet of the opposite hills. "Thet's him! Thet's Red Cloud!" The half-breed, his eyes for once shining wildly, couldn't keep the excitement out of his voice. "Now ye'll see somethin', Murphy! Watch them come, now! Look at thet! God!"

Come they did, whooping and hii-yeeing down on the empty camp, the thunder of their ponies' hoofs rolling across the valley like the drum-fire of wheel-locked artillery. Sergeant Murphy took one look before he jumped and ran for the rear. "Holy Mither of Mary, lookit them heathen bastirds ride!" Too much the old cavalryman, Murdo Murphy, even in such a moment, not to admire the great Sioux horsemanship.

Perez watched the howling Oglala hit the camp. The first wave rode right over the site, firing, blind, into the tents. Those would be American Horse's picked group of forty, containing every serviceable rifle the Oglala possessed. The second, main body of the Sioux haunch-slid their mounts to a dust-showering cloud of stops in among the tents, piling off the ponies and diving in through the tent flaps, intent on knifing and clubbing whatever soldiers survived the rifle charge.

In a matter of seconds they discovered the hoax, the camp then becoming a scene of utmost confusion. The Indians milled their ponies among the trampled tents, many still jamming their lances through tents or piles of duffel, hoping to find some hidden trooper. Scores of others were running about on foot among the supply dumps, hungrily plying the repacious Sioux appetite for loot. Half a dozen chiefs surrounded Red Cloud, gesturing and arguing heatedly.

Watching them, Perez knew he had a rare opportunity for an Indian-shoot. He also knew Red Cloud wouldn't be long figuring where the troops would have had to go to. If Murphy would only move his Irish ass fast enough, a man could put a charge of carbine-stitching into Makhpiya's blanket that would have the Oglala pulling red threads out of their butts for the next six moons.

45

"All set, Perez!" the sergeant's cheerful voice came out of the scrub to the scout's right.

"Hey, ye, Moriarity!" the half-breed's words cracked with tension. "Ye all set over thar?"

Moriarity's answer came popping from the brush to the left, echoing Murphy's optimism. "All set! Say the word, General!"

"All right. Hyar goes a three-count fer a volley. Fire on the count, then fire free. One. Two. Three!" The volley crashed out, followed by a wild piling of free shots. The new Spencer carbines were accurate, the men behind them unexpectedly cool for green replacements.

Several ponies went down, kicking and screaming. Others broke loose, running riderless down the valley. The hostiles, after a minute's mad scrambling, raced for the cover of the west grove. Many of them went riding double, the double riders in most cases hanging over the ponies' withers like very sick men. A ragged fire from Collins' troopers followed them but the range was too great. No more ponies went down as the savages got safely back to the trees.

"Chee-rist!" bawled Sergeant Moriarity, disgust in every rich tone, "we didn't git a single one of the bastirds. Lookit there! There ain't a body layin' in thet camp!"

"They never leave no bodies layin' around," called Perez. "Ye got some of them, all right. Eleven by my count."

"Hooray!" yelled Sergeant Murphy. "We'll give them red heathens a sweat, now!"

"Happen ye're wrong as a rat kissin' a cat, Murphy," Perez corrected, dourly. "They're goin' to hand us one. And they ain't aimin' to wait all week about workin' the lather up. Look over thar—" The two sergeants followed his pointing finger. Up out of the west grove, two long files of gaudily feathered warriors were climbing into the backing hills, one file winding south, the other north.

"Jasus! They're goin'!" Moriarity was jubilant.

"Not quite, Sergeant," Perez shook his head, "they're comin'! Around the valley, Moriarity. One column each way, behind the hills."

"Whut do yez reckon they're up to?" Murphy's question came uneasily.

"Some of them'll git up on the bluffs above our grove, here. The rest'll sneak out in the grass on our front and flanks. We'll likely take some hits from them but we're not in bad shape—if we keep cool and they don't rush us."

46

"Yez reckon they will rush us?"

"I reckon." The half-breed's answer was a flat statement of certainty. "A ordinary Injun wouldn't but Red Cloud ain't ordinary. He'll come after us. I only wisht I knew *how* he allowed to go about it, that's all. I ain't worryin' none about him tryin' it."

"Whut happens when he does?" Moriarity's query was husky with the kind of throat constriction common to white soldiers cornered ten-to-one by red hostiles. Perez didn't answer. There wasn't much a man could say to that question. Leastways not anything calculated to do any morale raising. Sergeant Murphy, on the other hand, felt compelled to offer his countryman some manner of solace.

"Well now, Sargint Moriarity, me fine, skinny buckoo, whut kind of posies will yez be after wantin'? And whut'll I be tellin' that fine widdy woman of yerz back in Fort Lorin'? Aye, 'tis a poor, sad colleen she'll be, my bye, with yer back all bristly with Sioux errers and yer fine sandy scalp abouncin' along on Rid Clowd's belt. Ah, but faith, Danny, Murphy's the lad to cheer her up. Never yez fear fer thet."

"Ye black Irish scut"—Moriarity's Hibernian pedigree was as clean as the meadow turf of Donegal—"I'll live to bury the likes of ye fourteen times over. And as fer Kathleen, Murdo me lad, ye ain't the boy fer the chore. She's used to a man with somethin' big besides his mouth."

"Kathleen won't have to worry about either of ye," broke in Perez, "if ye don't git to shootin' off somethin' besides yer flannel mouths. We've got company comin'."

Out in front the sergeants could see the grass moving where the scout nodded. "Git back to yer men. Tell them not to fire at movin' grass. Only at gun flashes and parts of Injuns they see red and clean. Murphy—" Perez called the sergeant back. "Whut's become of Lieutenant Collins?"

"The last I saw of him, the gurl was arguin' with him back there agin the cliff where yez put 'em. I think she's doin' like yez told her, tryin' to keep the lieutenant back there out of the way. But I doubt she's goin' to keep the lad quiet vurry long. He's a long ways from sober, yet. I still think yez ought to let me tie him up, Perez lad."

"No." The half-breed's answer was flat. "Thet'd be insultin' injury. He's hurt enough as it is, and he's goin' to make enough trouble for all of ye if we git him out'n hyar alive. I mean about me and ye and Moriarity runnin' his command out from under him. As it is, ye kin say he didn't make no effort to take

47

over. Ye tie him up and ye ain't even got thet left to say."
Murphy nodded, knowing damn well the strange, Indian-look-
ing scout had it figured on the bellybutton. He started to
answer Perez, but the latter cut in on him.

"And besides, we got all the trouble we kin handle without
we go to frettin' about Collins." Verifying the soft claim, the
sibilant hissing of arrows began to slant down through the
trees around them.

"*Aii-eee!*" the half-breed drew the words in between his
teeth, "thet means Red Cloud has got American Horse and
his rifles out front in the grass," he began, then broke his own
thought, "or does it, by Cripes? Say, listen, Sergeant, I've got
a hunch. Ye see how these cliffs bulge out into the valley?
With our grove sittin' on the bulge like a nipple on a swole tit?
Whut's to keep a bunch of horsemen from comin' around thet
bulge to git up on either side of us? We couldn't see the red
sons till they was within sixty yards of us."

"Ye're right!" Murphy was paying very soldierly attention,
now, as Perez went on.

"Them ain't riflemen out in thet grass, they're decoys. Ye'll
see. They won't fire a thing but mebbe a couple of old muzzle-
loaders or ball pistols."

"Whut'll we do?"

"Git Moriarity up agin the cliffs on one flank, yerse'f on the
other. When them horsemen come in—"

"I got yez," nodded the Irishman. "When they come in we
hold our fire till they're close up. Then we unload and knock
their heathen butts loose."

"Thet's it. Git a move on."

When it came, the interrupting voice jumped them both,
snarling out its words. "You're not going any place, Murphy!"

Perez and the sergeant wheeled to see Lieutenant Collins
swaying on braced feet, curly hair hanging limp, face flushed,
eyes red-rimmed and wild. Gesturing toward Perez with the
long cavalry Colt in his right hand, the officer slurred un-
steadily. "No red-skinned son of a squaw bitch is going to steal
my command. By God, I'll—"

Perez didn't try to talk, he just went for him. Collins fired
blindly but the scout was in under the flash, driving his right
arm up, fast. The clenched fist, gourd-big and hard as horn,
was ahead of an arm and shoulder tough as a pack mule's
off hind leg. Collins' head flipped back with a cracked-branch
snap. He hit the ground hard and lay still.

"It's a terrible thing to strike an officer," breathed Murphy, white-faced.

"Git to yer men!" The white teeth flashed in the dark face. "If American Horse gits into us around them cliffs ye'll find out how to spell turrible, soon enough."

"Yes, sir," assented the sergeant, backing away with an automatic salute. "But, faith, I hate to think of losin' me sergeant's stripes again. I've had 'em back fer two whole years, now."

"Take yer pick," grunted Perez. "Stripes or hair. It don't make me no never-mind, neither way."

"Yez have an imposin' point there, Mister Perez," admitted Murphy, heading for the brush. "Moriarity! Moriarity! Where the devil are yez, yez bog-trottin' Donegal scut—" The voice faded with the grin Perez sent after it.

A twig snapped behind the half-breed and he whirled to see the green-eyed Clanton girl standing beyond the fallen lieutenant. In her hands was a Spencer. "Here," she said, holding the carbine out to him, "it's his. I see he won't be needing it. What did you do to him? Is he dead?"

Perez took the weapon, levering it to check the magazine. There was something about the quiet way the girl watched him, the complete disregard she showed for the unconscious Collins, that upset the scout.

"He ain't dead," growled Perez, then added, challenge in the statement, "Ye don't seem too mightily disturbed about yer husband, ma'am."

"I don't care what happens to him. Or to me, either. I've been a fool." Her expression was unsmiling but her strange, almond-shaped eyes were beginning to heat in a way that set Perez' breath to catching. A man could look at a woman like this and think of a lot of things—all of them to do with getting his hands on that body and his teeth into that neck. The girl went on, her words jamming a curb bit hard between the jaws of the half-breed's champing thoughts, "He's not my husband. We were never married. I joined up with him in St. Louis without benefit of even thinking about clergy. I found out he was detailed to my father's command, and worked on him to bring me along. It wasn't hard. It never is with men. I thought we'd be married at Fort Loring but by that time I'd found out what kind of a weakling he was." The words, with the green eyes behind them, went straight into Perez' narrowed glance. "I'm sorry, Mister Perez. This whole damn mess is my fault."

49

"Wal, ma'am"—Perez shifted uncomfortably—"we all make mistakes. If ye want to fergit yers, ye've come to the right country. As fur as I'm concerned ye're Missus Collins, if that's the way ye want it."

"Thank you, Perez." The girl said it simply, her eyes never leaving the dark face. "We'll leave it that way for the others. For you, I'm Lura Clanton."

The tall half-breed heard the words, refused to admit their spine-straightening implication. In the world he'd known, a white girl didn't talk to a Pawnee breed like that.

"Right now, ma'am," the words were an order, "I want ye should go back agin the cliffs whar I put ye, and I want ye should stay thar. We're goin' to have it flung at us hot and heavy around hyar."

Lura Clanton looked at him with a directness no man could miss. "I'm going with you. I like you and I like it hot and heavy."

Perez felt the blood pile thick in his temples, pounding like scalp-dance drums. What the devil did she mean? This creamily beautiful white woman couldn't possibly—

"Do ye mean thet?" His hot stare swept her with a heat lightning flash.

"I mean it," was all she said.

The half-breed stepped over the unconscious lieutenant and seized her. One arm went around her waist, the crook of the other cupped her white neck viciously. It was a long, hard kiss, and the girl came into Perez with it, like fire sucking into a piece of dry wood.

When she twisted her mouth away from his, a thin line of blood ran from the full lower lip. "Let me go," her words were strangled, angry. "I can't breathe."

Perez moved away from her, his arms and all the muscles of his lean belly strung bow-tight with the cords of suppression. When she spoke again, he watched her eyes.

"I didn't mean *that*," she murmured, resentfully. "Not what you thought. Oh, Perez, I'm sorry!"

He watched her another moment before turning away. "Let's go. Ye meant it, all right." She didn't answer, and together they went through the trees back towards the cliffs, the girl following the man, her cat's-paw lightness of foot almost as neat and sure as his.

Behind them, Second Lieutenant Wilke Collins lay alone, his only company the whispering of the war arrows probing the grove with their flicking, nervous fingers.

Where it based up against the bluffs, the grove was perhaps forty yards wide. Perez lay on the north flank with Moriarity and his half of the troop. Murphy and the other half of the troop crouched thirty yards away, on the south flank.

A minute stretched itself nervously to five, then ten. Half an hour went by. Still no attack.

Perez cursed the wily Red Cloud. It appeared the War Chief figured he had all day to get them, would let them dangle on the hook, knowing full well the tension each minute's delay caused. The attack might come in five seconds or ten hours. This was Makhpiya Luta's advantage. He would enjoy it to the last nerve-twitch.

The sun was climbing now, beating into the thick foliage of the grove with the force of a molten hammer. The scout guessed an hour and a half had passed since he aroused the sleeping camp. If he hadn't lost the main trail or tried any short cuts, Stacey could show up within the next thirty minutes. That he would not, impetuous and green as he was, lose the Virginia City track was a longer gamble than Perez would worry about. Such as it was, however, the possibility that Stacey might show in Red Cloud's rear was the half-breed's advantage, the latter getting, in turn, what enjoyment he could from it. A man could always hope. If Makhpiya would just keep on stalling—

But the War Chief was through stalling. The assault came now and it came in such a way as to catch even the wary Perez off guard.

The scout had been waiting for the usual preludes to an Indian attack, the owl hoots, fox barks, bird calls and other nature sounds by which the red men habitually talked back and forth over the uncomprehending heads of their intended white victims. Even after these sounds there was always the last-second warning: the screaming war-whoops which inevitably preceded the frantic, rapid-fire galloping of the ponies' hoofs. But Red Cloud had heard a wolf howl just before he had raced down on the empty camp. The others had thought it was a wolf, but Makhpyia Luta had not been sure. Now, he was sure. He was sure it had not been.

Perez had turned to say something to Moriarity, taking his eyes from the front along the bluffs for a second's fraction. The next he felt was the tremble of the ground under him. Whirling, he saw fifty or sixty warriors already halfway across the open, no sounds issuing from their clamped mouths, their ponies straining their flying bellies to the grasstops. In their lead came American Horse, his careening black stallion easily marked among the piebald and motley horses of his followers.

"How about it, chief?" asked Moriarity, cool as a butter-pat in a wellhouse. "They're pretty close."

"Go ahaid," said Perez, levering his own Spencer into American Horse's black stud as he spoke.

"Fire!" yelled Moriarity, the twenty Spencers crashing so close on the word as to cover it. At such point-blank range the effect was very pretty. At least fifteen horses went down, including, of course, since Perez had pulled on him, American Horse's black.

The other riders came on, right over the neighing, kicking scramble of their companions' fallen mounts. They were within ten yards of Moriarity's men when the second volley came into them, and the third right on top of that.

Down went another clotted tangle of horses and riders, and still the hostiles came on. Half a dozen actually careened their ponies into and through the hard-firing troopers. But the others, about thirty of them, had had theirs. Turning, they swept off to the left, out into the open valley. The six warriors who got into the position lasted long enough to down four troopers, Sergeant Moriarity among them.

"Hold yer fire!" yelled Perez to the soldiers still shooting after the fleeing hostiles. "Let them go. Keep yer eyes on the ones we've got down out hyar along the bluffs. Thar's some injured out thar, playin' possum. Fire into every body ye kin see, whether it looks daid or not." As he talked the half-breed was callously following his own instructions. Proving his contention, some of the "dead" warriors began to crawl or struggle away. Carefully, the troopers shot these, one by one.

When there were no more "crawlers" Perez called out sharply, "All right, hold it. Git these injured back in the trees. Whar's thet girl? Oh, all right, ma'am. Take care of these men, See whut ye kin do for them. Never mind the sergeant, he's did fer." The scout turned on a tall Tennessean whose carbine had been hotter than a two-dollar pistol during the recent scrape. "Ye, thar! Take over hyar. And keep yer eyeballs skinned. I'm goin' over to see whut happened to Murphy."

"Yeah," drawled the trooper, "go ahaid. Reckon Ah cain handle this side foh a spell."

Perez bent over Sergeant Moriarity. The latter lay where he'd gone down, knees drawn up to his chest, hands pressed into his stomach. "In the belly, eh, Sergeant?" The dying man moved his head. "We ain't goin' to try and move ye," the scout said, softly. "I saw ye git it. I allow ye know whar yer number is."

"It's 'up,' chief." Moriarity got out a white smile with the words. "I ain't got no more guts left than a sick cat. Tell Murphy—" Perez could hear the teeth grind as they clamped to keep the blood from coming through. "Tell Murphy not to wipe his nose on any more poison ivy."

"I'll tell him," said Perez, and went quickly away. Sergeant Moriarity didn't hear the scout's agreement. Didn't see him get up and go away. His relaxing hands fell away from the sodden jacket front. He turned a little on one side, vomited, lay still.

Perez had heard Murphy's men firing all the while Moriarity's, on his side, were repulsing American Horse. He soon found the Irishman had had it fairly easy.

"They come in a big wave," Murphy began. "Didn't seem to have many guns. Must of bin a couple hunderd of them but they was jest firin' bows and errers. We give them two volleys and they veered off acrost the valley. I think I seen Rid Clowd, Big scut, ridin' a paint studhorse?"

"Yeah, thet's him. The old coyote fooled me. Didn't split up his rifles none. Sent American Horse and all the guns in on our side. Near got us, too. He's a cute weasel's whelp, I don't mean jest mebbeso. We lost Moriarity and three men wounded."

"Moriarity?" Murphy's question was slow with apprehension. "Not Danny Moriarity? There's anither Moriarity over there wid yez, yez know. One of the troopers, a bye named Kivvin. Maybe—"

"*Your* Moriarity," said the half-breed, unfeelingly. "Sergeant Moriarity."

"Aw, no," the tears sprang unashamed to course down the sun-cracked cheeks, "not me bye, Danny."

"In the gut," nodded Perez. "He died quick."

Murphy was silent, looking off across the empty grasslands. Perez watched him and knew that the old sergeant was seeing plenty far off. A man didn't have to be a medicine dreamer to tell when another man was back-traveling the travois ruts of memory's trail. Only in Murphy's case they wouldn't be travois ruts. They'd be shod horse tracks running in lines of four, and troops of forty. The Irishman's voice was burred with softness, but the tears were gone. "Did he say anythin', now, before he went?"

53

"Yeah. He said to tell ye not to wipe yer nose on any more poison ivy."

"Ah, me nose, indeed," murmured Murphy, wistfully. "The little scut once handed me a fistful of poison ivy when I asked him like a gentleman fer a waddin' of sawft grass. 'Twas a dirty Irish trick and the saints preserve us, I was the talk of the latrine fer six weeks, hand-runnin'. 'Twas claimed yez could read the fine print on an Arbuckle's coffee bag in the dark, jest by the glow of Murphy's terrarrah. Me nose, indeed. Bless the bye's little heart." Murphy sniffed lugubriously in conclusion. "Well, anyway, we put a spoke in the red heathins' wheel thet'll have them runnin' lopsided fer a week of fish days. When do yez figure them to come back, Perez lad?"

"Take a look out thar and figure it fer yerse'f," Perez gestured, grimly.

Murphy looked and saw a long line of warriors approaching them from across the valley. There were a couple of hundred of them spread out five yards apart, making a bent sickle over half a mile long. A dozen chiefs rode the line, issuing war cries and battle orders, wholesale. Conspicuous among them, Makhpiya Luta, Red Cloud, the War Chief, wheeled and dodged his nervous pinto.

"Those are the ones we just run off," growled Perez. "Now look down thar," pointing south with a sudden, stabbing sweep of his arm.

"Heaven help us! Anither hunderd of them!"

"Yeah, and thar'll be a hunderd more on my side. They've come down off'n the bluffs."

"Faith, ye're right. There ain't no more errers comin' down."

"Thet accounts fer all four hunderd of them," added Perez, thoughtfully. "And by the way they're fixin' to come at us, I'd say they'll git us this try." There was no despair in the statement, only bone-dry opinion with none of the meat of damnfoolery hung on it.

"Do yez really think so, Perez?"

"Hell, yes. They're goin' to make a big rush, now. They's thirty-eight of us in hyar, four hunderd of them out thar. Carbines or no carbines, if they come at us without breakin', our meat's roasted."

"Where do yez suppose Major Stacey is hidin' his smilin' bye-ish face, right now?"

"Who the hell knows? He's due afore now, providin' he ain't lost hisse'f, which he likely has. He minds me of a hound dog runnin' a trail with his nose up his own tin-hole. There

54

ain't much doubt he seen yer camp smokes early this mornin', same as me and Red Cloud. But I allow either me or the War Chief kin run a smoke down summat smoother'n Major Stacey, if ye foller me."

"Hell, I follow yez—" Murphy began, but Perez cut him, quick, his voice suddenly low and fast.

"Murphy, spread yer men around this edge of the grove. Spread them clean around till they meet up with Tennessee's. I'll see thet he gits his spread to cover the other side. I got the hostiles figured to come in from the front and both flanks. All we kin do is spread out thin to cover the whole edge of the grove. Tell yer boys to keep firin' low, aimin' to git the hosses down. Don't fire at the riders till they're thet close in ye kin spit on the bastards. Pound thet into their haids, understand? Keep blastin' away till the Injuns are right on top of ye. An Injun will nine times out'n ten break his charge close up if the fire keeps comin' into him and gittin' his hosses down. They cain't stand up to it close in like a white man kin. They jest don't cotton to it in their guts, not no-ways. Above all, start gittin' them hosses down while they're still far out. A Plains Injun 'thout a hoss under him ain't no more use nor a puff of butt-gas in a whirlygust."

"Yes sir, anythin' else?"

"Nope, jest remember when they do git close in, don't hold high fer head or shoulder shots. In the guts, Murphy. Ye got thet?"

"Yes sir, I got it. And so did Moriarity. I'll remember thet, Perez, and I'd like to shake yer hand. Ye're a first-class fightin' man, red or white."

"All right, Sergeant." The half-breed gripped the old soldier's orange-haired paw, knowing from the pressure of it and from the earnest squint of the blue eyes behind it, what all men know who've been there: that when the last raise has been made and called, all men are the same color. "Good luck, Murphy. Remember all I told ye."

The men parted, each going at a lope, back through the woods.

Perez got Tennessee and his men spread, ordering them to hold their fire till the Indians were two hundred yards out. Looking around, he saw nothing of the girl, nor of Lieutenant Collins. A drawling voice spoke at his side. "Ah reckon they'll fry our fat foh us, this time." The big Tennessean levered a shell into his Spencer as he talked.

"Yeah, and about all we kin do is spatter as much of it on

55

them as we kin, while they're fryin' it." As the half-breed spoke, the approaching red lines neared two hundred yards and a single warrior rode out of the leading group. He was a lean, dark-hued Sioux, garbed in black buckskin leggins, wearing a solitary spotted eagle feather slanting through his braids. When he saw him, Perez' breath came sucking in sharp as an arrow's hiss. "*Hookahey!* I was afeard so!"

"What's the matter?"—this, tensely, from Tennessee.

"Thet's him."

"Who?"

"American Horse—the one in the black leggins. The son of To-Ke-Ya has more lives then a six-toed cat. I allowed mebbe I got him when I knocked his hoss out from under him. Shoulda knowed better."

"Wal, let's see if we cain't git about nine of them lives away from him," grinned the lanky mountaineer. "Ah feel right lucky."

"Ye've got yer chancet to push thet luck a morsel, right now," annuonced Perez.

Across the valley, Red Cloud threw his carbine up, firing it four times. "Thet's the signal," barked the half-breed. "Four's their good-luck medicine number. Hyar they come."

The hostiles broke in a running wave toward the grove. "The boys are shootin' right well," commented Tennessee, as the Indian ponies began to go down, hock over fetlock, all along the charging line. But even as the hill private spoke, and with the range shortening to a hundred yards, the fire going out from the grove slackened appreciably.

"I'll kiss yer butt till it barks like a blue fox," snarled Perez, lowering his carbine to listen. "How do ye like them apples?"

"Yeah," groaned his companion, at the same time throwing down his own carbine and pulling a long bowie knife from inside his jacket, "it's the damn ammunition. Mine's gone, too."

With a wry grin, the hill man turned to Perez, watching the latter, bright-eyed, calmly awaiting his next move. "I hate to think ye're right," the half-breed's rare grin flashed, "but I allow ye are. Kind of slows a man down, too, not havin' no more rocks to throw."

Tennessee spat on the bowie's broad blade, wiped it on his greasy buckskin leggins, consoled Perez laconically. "Wal, ye done a good job while ye laisted, mistuh. Ye fought like a swamp cat with a coon dawg in a holler stump. Say, now, pahdnuh, do ye reckon thet's Gabriel's trumpet I hear blowin'?" The question was the kind of iron joke a man will put out

56

when he figures the last chip has been shoved into the middle of the blanket.

In this case, Perez missed the humor—for good and sufficient cause. A trumpet *was* blowing.

"It may sound like Gabe to ye," he grimaced, "but it fer jure listens like Major Stacey to me!"

"Wal, Ah'll be a hind-tit pig! The U. S. Cavalry to the rescue!" The mountaineer's words were no less fervent for their sarcasm. "Man, oh man, ye cain say all ye want to, but a troop of hoss comin' thetaway, with the guidons flyin' and the bugler blowin' butt off, is really somethin'!"

Perez, watching Stacey's galloping troop coming across the valley, felt compelled to go along with the larger sentiments of his companion's heartfelt utterance. A man couldn't very well look at those thirty blue-uniformed white men lathering their horses down on top of better than four hundred howling redskins, without gtting the goosy-flesh of pride bumping up along his backbone high enough to mount a pony from. Outnumbered or not, there was something about the way the crazy white bastards were coming hammering in at the Sioux that made it look as if they thought the thirty of them could handle four thousand hostiles.

Others, apparently, were getting the same impression.

Forty yards short of the grove, Red Cloud swung wide, his part of the battle line following him, to head south and downvalley. The rest of the Sioux, sweeping around the grove from its north side, streamed off after him.

" 'Pears my red cousins agree with ye, Tennessee," commented the half-breed scout, allowing himself the luxury of a half-smile.

" 'Pears they do," the hill man grinned back.

Well earned as those smiles were, they were premature. The forgotten Lieutenant Collins chose the instant of their spreading across the faces of Perez and Tennessee to make his belated and final contribution to the day's disasters.

As Perez spoke to Tennessee, he was startled to see the disheveled figure of Lieutenant Collins burst from the cover of the woods about thirty yards to his right. The officer was stumbling and running out into the open grasslands, waving his arms and shouting to the approaching Stacey, still a quarter of a mile away across the valley.

"Help us! For God's sake, help us!" he screamed, voice wild and hoarse with hysteria. "We're being shot to pieces!"

57

"He's out'n his haid!" cried Tennessee, leaping to his feet. "Ah'm goin' out aftuh him."

Perez grabbed the mountaineer, shoving him down, hard. "Git down. Ye cain't go out thar. Collins is not only out'n his haid, he's goin' to be out'n his scalp, too. Lookit thar!" Following the scout's pointing gesture, Tennessee cursed, softly.

"Mah Gawd. Ah thought they was all gone."

Coming from the north side of the grove, at a belly-stretching gallop, the riders straining far over their mount's lathered necks, a last group of Sioux charged around the edge of the woods. Lieutenant Collins heard the rush of ponies' hoofs and possibly the first two or three shots, no more. A literal blast of rifle fire knocked him sprawling, face forward, arms flopping grotesquely, into the long grass. Perez and Tennessee were so close they could see the dust-puffs fly from the crazed officer's jacket as the Sioux lead ripped into him.

"Lawd Gawd A'mighty," breathed the mountain man, "they sho weighted him down foh the big jump."

"He picked a *Hopo* time to go fer a trot," growled Perez, tersely. "Thet was American Horse's bunch he tied into."

"Whut do ye suppose ailed him to go runnin' out thetaway?"

"I dunno," the half-breed's answer was short. "Happen a man'll do many a funny thing oncet his nerves git pickled in whiskey and he's had his pride humbled."

The Sioux had now disappeared downvalley, and Stacey, who had switched off to chase them a ways, was coming trotting back up the meadow.

"Ah guess the poh devil's done foh," said Tennessee, scanning the grass where Collins had fallen. "Ah don't see no movin' around out theah."

"Wal," observed his companion, the words so dry you expected them to puff dust, "if he's aimin' to die anyways, I hope he's done already made it."

"Yeah, Ah reckon ye do. One of the boys was tellin' me ye done slugged the lieutenant back theah in the woods."

"Had to. He didn't leave me no choice. Plumb wild. Tried to gun me down."

"Ennybody see it?"

"Murphy."

"Ye're plain lucky. The sergeant'll back ye up. He's got moh guts then a Guv'ment mule."

"We'll see sudden enough. Hyar comes the cavalry!"

Watching Stacey ride up, Tennessee drawlingly opined,

"Nevah did like thet offisuh. Lookit the little cock rooster fluffin' his feathahs. Man, he's done a'ready give hisse'f credit foh savin' ouh outfit."

"Let's git a blanket and go bring Collins in," Perez made the suggestion, abruptly. "He could be alive."

"Sho, I'll git the wrapper. Be baick in a minute."

A few seconds later, bending over Collins' body, Tennessee muttered, "Yer tough luck, mistuh. He's still breathin'."

"Mebbe his wick'll sputter afore we git him in," said Perez, casually. "Roll him in the blanket easy-like. He's so full of holes ye could read week-old trail sign through him." The scout's optimism was ill founded. Collins lived long enough to talk.

Perez and Tennessee had no more than gotten the moribund lieutenant into the blanket than Stacey cantered up. "It's a long trail that leads nowhere, Indian," he sneered cheerily to the scout. "It looks like you'll still make that courtmartial. That's Lieutenant Collins, isn't it?"

"It's him," shrugged the scout, "but it won't be, long."

Dismounting, Stacey slid his arm behind the dying man's neck, propping him half up. "Collins, can you hear me? Can you talk, man?"

The youth's eyelids flickered and Stacey shouted to his sergeant. "Bring me a canteen, Jensen. Hurry up!"

When he had the container, he sloshed the contents over the lieutenant's head. "Come on, Collins, brace up, man. I've got to know what went on here. Can you hear me, Lieutenant? I'm Major Stacey. I want you to tell me what happened here." Collins nodded, weakly, the words coming with a rush when they began.

"I had a good camp out in the valley. Just before dawn an Indian came into my tent. He said he was an Army scout with Colonel Clanton. Said we were surrounded by hostile Sioux and had to get out. I thought the whole thing was a trick . . . refused to go. He knocked me down . . . put a knife in me . . . forced me to crawl over here . . . made Lura do it, too . . . on her hands and knees, like a damn animal. I—"

"Lura!" Stacey's interruption was tense. "Lura Clanton? Colonel Clanton's girl?"

"Lura Collins," the young officer made his dying bid for decency, "my wife." Perez nodded grimly, watching Stacey.

The words hit the cavalryman like a sledge, but he took them without breaking his stride. The half-breed, eyes narrowing, made a mental note that the major might be a fool, but a damn tough one, that was for certain. Stacey's words let Perez know the officer could see old Yunke-lo standing alongside Collins. "Go on, Lieutenant. Hurry up, man. Then what?"

"The next thing I remember, we were here in these trees and the Sioux were attacking. I was still confused from the blow the Indian spy had given me in the tent. When my mind cleared, I tried to take over my command. He knocked me unconscious. When I came around again, I got up to the edge of the woods. I'd been disarmed while unconscious and I found Murphy taking orders from the Indian. I didn't know what to do. I was afraid the crazy Indian would come at me again. Then I saw the Sioux turning off and you coming across the valley. I started to run out to meet you, and—" Collins' head fell back over Stacey's arm. The major's free hand jerked the head back up, sharply.

"Collins! Collins, can you hear me? Dammit, come on, man! Can you hear me?"

"He cain't hear nobody," Perez' soft voice broke the answering silence. "He's daid. *Mani Wakan Tanka.*"

Stacey laid the body back on the blanket, stood up to face the half-breed. "Yes, Indian, he's dead. Thank God, he lived long enough to take you with him. You'll hang, now, Perez. You should have settled for the Dry Tortugas."

"Ye're cracked as a porcelain piss-pot," shrugged the scout. "Collins was drunk on duty, had bin fer days. He couldn't command his own laigs, let alone a troop of horse."

"You lying red bastard!" Stacey's gloved hand came across the half-breed's face, slashing viciously.

Perez didn't move. A man didn't have to be real brainy to know how he stood as a lone "Indian" among white Army troops. Nor to figure that if Stacey could make Collins' yellow-belly charges stick, he'd do it. The scout knew, too, that the next few minutes could mean the difference between freedom and getting his tonsils wedged in a hemp clamp. The half-breed's wide mouth stayed shut as a sprung trap.

"The lieutenant was drunk," Tennessee spoke unexpectedly, with labored slowness, knowing his words marked him for insubordination, "jest like Mistuh Perez said."

"Private!" Stacey's command came, barking-quick. "You can air your views at the trial. Meanwhile you'll keep your mouth shut. You and every man in your troop. Sergeant Jensen, disarm this man and put him under guard." Stacey wheeled from Tennessee, stabbing his finger at Perez. "We'll attend to him when Clanton comes up. And this time, by God, we'll have our drumhead court-martial!"

"Ye kin have yer court-martial, I'll take the woods," drawled Perez easily. "Let's git back in thar afore Red Cloud realizes the infantry ain't right back of yer ass. I know thet Injun. He'll be back the minute he savvies thar's no support followin' ye."

Stacey started to turn angrily on the scout, but his action was interrupted by a bellowing shout from the grove. "Yez better git yer men under cover, Major! Rid Clowd is comin' back up the valley!" The dust cloud rolling with the galloping Indian ponies was clincher enough for Murphy's warning. The major's men scattered for the trees like a quail covey stomped on by six bird dogs.

Once in the grove, Stacey took the command, first ordering Perez securely bound. Sergeant Murphy, panting up to get his orders, was in time to see the troopers seize and bind the scout. "Beggin' yer pardon, Major, but yez better let him have a gun till the shootin's over. He's handier with a Spencer than a nigger with a new knife. I—"

"You better worry about yourself, Sergeant. Lieutenant Collins accused you of outright insubordination."

"Yes, sir," Murphy saluted the admission. "He was drunk, poor bye, may God rest his soul."

By now the Sioux were racing back and forth across the front of the woods, riding and firing wildly. At the same time the rate of fire going out from the grove was growing heavier. The Indians couldn't seem to agree on a charge. American Horse, the implacable, along with about a hundred braves, started in once only to veer sharply off while still well out.

The hostiles now drew off a good five hundred yards, milling and wheeling around in obvious argument. While they palavered, a high dust cloud became visible five miles west—squarely over the line of the Virginia City Road.

Red Cloud showed hesitation, and as he did, three riders came whooping down out of the hills, fanning their lathered ponies across the valley toward the waiting War Chief. Seconds after their arrival, the hostile band departed eastward, for the Powder, their pace such as to indicate the three scouts had reported Clanton's double-time approach.

An hour later, Clanton marched in with his musicians blowing the daylights out of "Garry Owen" and his supply, ammunition and baggage wagons rumbling and banging impressively. A secure camp was set up, rations issued, the minor wounded cared for, Lieutenant Collins read under the ground. Following these duties Colonel Clanton and his daughter were in his tent for better than an hour.

It was early evening before Perez was brought before the commanding officer and Stacey presented the charges made by Collins: unauthorized seizure of a command in the field, assaulting an officer, responsibility for the casualties suffered by G Troop.

Sergeant Murphy was present under charges of insubordination and being an accessory to Perez' command seizure, with Tennessee along as a material witness. Lura Collins was present on her own invitation and under no charges save those repeated ones leveled by the appraising glances of Major Phil Stacey. The girl didn't miss the warm evidence of the officer's hotly wandering eyes, doing nothing more to encourage them than to return them with a direct, calculating stare which, to the watching Perez, seemed to do all but set the price of the assignation.

The half-breed didn't miss so much as an eyelash tremble of this optical conversation, but what emotion it might be creating within him wasn't visible in the narrow, dark face. With his own fate hanging on the colonel's decision, Perez figured he had more immediate worries than the redheaded Clanton girl.

Withal, though, fiercely as he might close his mind to her, the scout was suffering. The memory of that smashing kiss over the unconscious form of Lieutenant Collins would not down. Never having been shot with the love arrow before, the Pawnee breed, even while feeling its deep twinge, failed to understand the nature of the wound. Women, sure. Lots of them. But that was crotch-cloth love. It had in no way whatever to do with the way Perez felt about this curving, white creature. Why, hell, just the smell of her was enough to make a man flare his nostrils wider than a four-year-old buffalo bull three feet downwind of an open heifer. Perez' eyes got that narrow you'd wonder how he could see out of them at all, and they never left Stacey.

The red-bearded major outlined his case with a great deal of earnest conviction, Colonel Clanton at once asking Perez for his story in rebuttal. The lean breed looked long and hard at Lura Collins, his simple, Indian's heart offered in the level gaze. The girl, wild and adventurous as she was, was as clean of actual love-lance scars as the half-breed, himself. Now, meeting his burning stare, her bold glance wavered and fell, her creamy skin flushing darkly. For one of the few times in his life, Perez misread obvious trail-sign, assuming the falling glance and rushing blood to spell "shame." Shame for what she was about to do—and that would be to sidle away from standing behind the scout's story.

He had counted on the girl, goddam it. She had seen the whole thing, right from the time he had entered Collins' tent. Now, looking at her, a man knew she wouldn't support his tale at the cost of exposing her own shameful role in the tragedy. Flicking his eyes to Colonel Clanton, the half-breed shrugged. "I have no story. My heart is bad. My tongue is dead. Let the others speak. White ears are uncovered only when white tongues speak." -

It was a bitter speech, coming from a red heart, through a red tongue, and following it Perez got the surprise of his life.

Tennessee told what had happened, his story being agreed to, in detail, by Murphy and the girl. The sergeant then told his story and, lastly, Lura Clanton, hers, her wide-eyed gaze on the somber scout the whole while, her words sparing nothing of her own shame, nor of his bravery.

Colonel Clanton sat for a long minute, his blue eyes studying the accused half-breed. When at last he spoke, his words opened Perez' slitted stare with amazement.

"It is obvious," the colonel announced, slowly, "that Lieutenant Collins was guilty of dereliction of duty. As a matter of routine we shall verify this testimony given just now with that of the rest of the troops, but to me it is quite plain we owe Pawnee Perez a debt of gratitude and that, far from castigating him for the precipitation of four casualties, we should congratulate him for the prevention of forty."

Turning to the half-breed, Colonel Clanton concluded, simply, "Pawnee, I want to thank you. There has been tragedy and disgrace enough here without our compounding them with baseless charges against the bravest man among us. I think thirty-eight men and a very lucky woman owe you their lives. That's a considerable debt and one I hope we all appreciate." With the words, his gaze found the uncomfortable Stacey, the latter being quick to gather the implication.

"Perhaps you're right, Colonel," the admission came reluctantly. "I don't believe this man but it would seem the evidence of a completely disinterested party, disinterested, that is, from the military responsibility standpoint, like Mrs. Collins"—here a gracious bow to the bereaved widow, who was at the moment affecting a coy humility which brought the quick wolf-grin to Perez' lips—"cannot be disregarded. It is clear from her testimony that Lieutenant Collins had been drinking. I'm ready to withhold judgment."

"The very least you might do, I should think, Major," gruffed Clanton, stiffly. "And now we'll close this inquiry. Perez is clear in the matter. And," the addition was a meaningful one, sent out with a nod to Stacey. "I want him treated that way."

The half-breed scout thanked the older man briefly and, as the others departed without further comment, asked permission to leave the camp.

"Of course," Clanton's consent was brisk and friendly, "you're free to do as you like. But, Pawnee, I'd like very much to have you stay on with me in the position of Chief Scout. That's a Government position, with the Army, officially, carrying a sergeant's stripes and three hundred dollars a month."

"I dunno, Colonel. It's a hard spot, me bein' a half—"

"Nonsense," Clanton broke in on his hesitation, "there's nothing to it. It's all too hard to find reliable men like yourself, who know the country and the Indians in it. You know I'm up here to build Fort Will Farney on the far side of the Powder. You also know that means 'trouble' in large letters. You'll have no difficulty earning your pay man, and I'm asking you, as one white man to another, to stay on here and help us build our fort. You've a job if you'll take it, John Perez." The final offer came wrapped in the colonel's frankest smile, was extended with the firm right hand he held forth to the listening half-breed.

As Perez started to decline the offer without serious consideration, his flinty eyes caught the figures of Major Stacey and Lura Collins. The two were standing by the officer's tent, Stacey talking animatedly, the girl smiling provocatively, apparently much taken with the major's dash of character.

But the minute Perez' vision found her, her eyes left the cavalryman's conversation, locking hard with the lean breed's glance.

Perez could feel that look go into him like a six-inch skinning knife. Ten minutes before he couldn't, for his scalp, have read the sign in that knife-glance. But love learns fast.

"Ye've got a scout," said the half-breed suddenly, his hand closing on Colonel Clanton's. "I need the money and ye're goin' to need a chaperon."

3 WASIYA

The Winter Giant

WITH PEREZ SCOUTING FOR HIM, COLONEL CLANTON MADE
a reconnaissance as far north as the Tongue River, searching
for a site upon which to build his fort. Finally, he selected
as bad a place as there was on the entire trail, a low-lying
flat in the Spruce Creek Fork of the Powder River. The surrounding hills pressed in close on the site, allowing the hostiles
to look down on Clanton's every move, preventing the latter
from seeing a thing.

Perez' arguments against the site and Colonel Clanton's
plans for it were so vehement the commander was forced to
remind the half-breed he was a scout, not a military consultant
or fellow engineer.

Perez was stubborn. The fort was five miles from good timber, all wood having to be hauled in through rough, dangerous
terrain. There were no decent hay meadows close in, all
fodder for the stock having to be freighted in from distant
sites. The plans for the fort did not include a stockade wing
enclosing a strip of adjacent Spruce Creek for fresh water
within the walls, an oversight which was to prove nigh dis-
astrous. Owing to the rugged surrounding country, there was
no way of mounting an effective guardpost system. Attacking
hostiles could sneak within pistolshot of the stockade without
being seen.

Colonel Clanton and his wild-eyed junior, Major Stacey,

smiled or scowled down all Perez' serious warnings. Clanton was an engineer, Stacey a cavalryman of reputation. This was their business.

And it was a fine fort, too, beautifully constructed, spacious, eight hundred by six hundred feet and, Perez thought, the most complete layout of its kind he'd ever seen. "The best fort in the West, in the worst place in the world," was the way he put it to John Creighton, a civilian scout hired by Clanton shortly after the work on the fort began, and the half-breed's only real friend on the post. There were two other scouts on the rolls, "Beaver" Burton O'Connor and "Dirty Charlie" Bailey, but they were weather-cracked old mountain men, taking a dim and distant view of "everythin' Injun," especially half-breeds.

Creighton, on the other hand, though a white man, was new to the frontier, eager to learn, fascinated by the Indians. He was a dark, taciturn man, well over six feet, extremely powerful, whose swart coloring and hawk's feature of face made him look more like a Sioux than most of the real articles Perez had known. Creighton was the finest natural shot the half-breed scout had ever seen, this skill soon gaining him the spot of post meat hunter, a duty which separated him and Perez much of the time. Such as their friendship was, however, it was the only actual one Pawnee had—though not quite the only one, at that.

Lura Collins remained warm and responsive, continuing to look at the scout with sufficient directness to buckle his knees as though somebody had belted him back of them with an ox yoke.

In Perez' place there was little time for Lura Collins, looks or not. All during its building, the fort was under constant attack by Red Cloud, necessitating the scout's being in the field night and day. His job was continually to rove the open country, reporting any concentration of hostiles large enough to spell a concerted attack on the fort.

No such concentration occurred, though every day brought some new Indian assault, either on one of the wood-cutting details sent out from the fort or on one of the emigrant trains which continued to pass up the Virginia City Road. During the three months of its construction, between seventy-five and eighty whites were killed. Nonetheless, December found the fort completed in detail, garrisoned to near capacity.

Clanton, again against the advice of his scouts, relaxed his original orders forbidding the officers to bring their families up from Fort Loring. Thus, the early winter which Perez had predicted so many months before would bring the big Sioux assault swarming under the first blizzard, found Fort Will Farney crawling not only with troops but with women and children as well.

Fifty miles to the north, the Sioux and Cheyenne war chiefs began gathering in the Wolf Mountains.

Red Cloud was there, and American Horse, with High-Hump-Back, Black Buffalo, Gray Bull and Elk Nation. These were all Sioux of reputation, but the Cheyenne lodges matched them, chief for chief. Young Two Moons, He Dog, Bob-Tail-Horse and Little Wolf were names to put the hard clamp of fear on the breathing of any white soldier or settler. Last to arrive, with two hundred lodges of Oglala Bad Faces, was a chief of name and reputation to shadow them all. It was this chief Perez spotted while running out a broad track of travois poles he'd crossed forty miles north and east of Fort Farney.

It was a brittle-cold December day, wine-clear and still as a buzzard's shadow. Perez, cutting the trail of the moving village about noon, had known at once that this was the first sign of the hostile concentration he'd been expecting.

A watcher, looking at Colonel Travis Clanton's senior scout studying that hostile travois track, would have seen a leathery-dark man, lean as a dried navel cord. Would have noted the narrow head moving constantly, the slant, black eyes never still, ceaselessly roving every quarter of the landscape. Would have thought that well might they move thus, those eyes upon whose chert-cold accuracy depended the lives and safety of the northernmost Army post along the bloody Virginia City Road.

The face which held those eyes was not the one to go well with an unwarned meeting in the dark.

It was a thin face, high-cheekboned, of skull-like sculpture, a short, spade beard pointing the long jaw. The mouth was as iron-lipped as a Cheyenne Dog Soldier's, a big mouth, a merciless mouth, an Indian mouth. The whole man went with the mouth. When you saw Pawnee Perez you thought of one thing: a lean, high-withered buffalo wolf, alert, nervous, dangerous.

Behind the half-breed, now, lay Fort Will Farney. In front of him, somewhere in the weird snow-tumble of the Wolf Mountains, must lie the suspected concentration of Sioux and Cheyenne hostiles which report had insisted was gathering there under Makhpiya Luta for the long-threatened wipe-out of the Little White Eagle Chief and his treaty-breaking, Powder River fort—the concentration whose existence and intent would be proved by the nature of the village the scout was now following. If that village were headed by the chief Perez figured it was—

All day he ran the travois trail out, coming an hour short of sunset, in sight of the distant, tenuous spirals of cooking-fire smokes.

Pausing briefly to let Sosi, his mud-yellow gelding, blow out, Perez studied the twisted land ahead, then, clucking softly, he put the little horse back on the trail.

Half an hour's catfooted going, up a side valley paralleling the village track, topped them out on a low ridge overlooking a sight which drew in the half-breed's breath with a whistle sharp as a Spencer's slug.

Below him spread some two hundred Oglala Sioux lodges, the peaceful smokes of their fires lazily wisping out of the tipi smoke-holes, crawling, blue-white, up into the thin air of the winter twilight. But it was not the number of the lodges that brought the scout's breath sucking in.

It was the pony herd.

Perez could tell you the identity of any sizable Sioux village by its horses. If he could see the horse herd, he could tell you whose village it was. He could see this horse herd. He knew those horses as you might your neighbor's dogs. Turning to Sosi, whose muzzle he held tight-wrapped, he whispered, "Ho, ye, Sosi! Do ye recognize yer friends down thar?"

The little buckskin flicked his ears nervously, his strange, grass-blue eyes watching the grazing animals below.

"Mebbe now we kin git old Iron-haid to uncover his ears!" Perez referred to Colonel Clanton. "Wait'll we tell him who's sneakin' into the Wolves with five hunderd warriors. *Aii-eee!*"

Swiftly, the half-breed worked his way off the back side of the ridge, hand-leading the yellow pony down the icy going. At the bottom he paused, as a keening wind whipped suddenly through the stillness of the gully. "Our Sioux friends across the ridge, thar, ain't the only ones thet's comin'," he muttered, removing the nose-wrap from the gelding's muzzle. "Do ye smell whut I smell, Sosi, old friend?" The horse threw his sooty nose into the freshening wind, snuffling softly, then lay his ears back, flatly, swinging his rump to the wind, hunching his back like a snow-drifted steer.

"Aye, ye smell it, all right. Thet's Wasiya, eh, Sosi?"

For answer the gelding hunched his back yet more, nudging the man with quick bunts of his black nose. *Wasiya* was the Sioux name of the Blizzard, the winter giant. *Wanitu* was Winter, but Wasiya was the Giant. He carried the big snows in his frozen chest.

"Let's make tracks far away from hyar, little hoss." The half-breed's words were grimly subdued. "Happen I don't like the smell of thet wind no more then I do the looks of thet camp."

The fort was dark when Perez galloped Sosi up to the stockade at 11 P.M. Sergeant Murdo Murphy was on the main-gate guard detail, the scout answering him abruptly when his challenge came down through the darkness.

"It's Perez. Open up!"

"Holy Sleepin' Mary," muttered the sergeant. "I was jest gittin' me beauty rest."

"Hope ye enjoyed it," called the scout, loping through the stockade gates. "Ye ain't goin' to git another fer some spell." Inside, he pulled the gelding up, dismounting.

"Whut's up, Perez?" frowned the Irishman, noticing Sosi's steaming flanks. "Faith, now, ye've ridden the poor little beast most to death."

"Yeah. I got to put him up and rub him off. While I'm doin' it, ye'd best roust the colonel out'n the hay. Tell him I've got somethin' thet'll curl his wig six ways from Sunday. Best git the other officers, too. He'll want them to hear this."

"Yes, sir!" answered Murphy, sensing an urgency not in the scout's actual words. "Right away."

"And git John Creighton over thar, too," Perez called after him. "*I'll* want him."

"Yez bet I will. I'll have the lot of them over there in three minutes."

Murphy was as good as his word. When Perez entered Fenton's office five minutes later, every officer on the post, except the O.D., was present: Major Stacey, Captain Benson, Captain Tendrake, another captain Perez didn't know, and the three lieutenants.

As the half-breed neared the C.O.'s office, a tall shadow loomed up through the darkness, the guttural voice of John Creighton coming growling with it. "Whut's in the wind, Pawnee?"

"A blizzard fer one thing, Hawk," Perez answered, using the name the admiring Sioux had given the other scout.*

"Ye're not ridin' thet muckle-dun pony of yers into a green lather jest to bring in a weather report." Creighton's words were dry as powder. "I kin smell thet snow same as ye. It's comin' and it's comin' big, but thet ain't whut's got yer nostrils flung wide."

"Ye're wrong." The wolf-grin flicked its twisted way across the swart features. "I got a blizzard to report, all right. Jest a shade different color than usual, thet's all."

"Color wouldn't be *red*, would it?"

"Ye damn betchy. We got a 'red blizzard' comin', ye kin tie yer stick on thet, Hawk."

"Ye sartain sure?"

"Sure's a schoolmarm's got a soft laig."

"Anybody we know?" The white scout's voice was that easy he might be asking the time of day.

"Tashunka," said the half-breed, turning for the colonel's door.

"*Aii-eee!*" breathed Creighton, softly, as the yellow light closed behind Perez.

Inside, Perez' report was as sure for short as it was far from sweet. Colonel Clanton was in a poor mood. He was a man who enjoyed the rigors of his own discipline, one of which was lights out at nine and a good ten hours' sleep. His statement to the scout was challenging.

"You'd better have something important, Perez. I don't like my garrison routed out in the middle of the night for no good reason."

"This is a fair-to-middlin' good reason," muttered the scout, "but ye sure as all hell won't like it. Tashunka Witko and five hunderd Oglala Bad Faces are camped forty miles north and east of hyar. They're headin' fer the Wolf Mountains. And uncover yer ears to this one, Colonel. When I give ye five hunderd Oglala, I'm talkin' about crotch-cloth Injuns. Thar ain't a squaw, nor a old man, nor a kid in thet camp, whut's figured in thet count. Thar's two hunderd lodges of them. I genrilly figure twixt two and three warriors to the lodge."

"Who the hell cares?" Major Stacey had been called away from company more glandularly attractive than that of his

---

* The hostiles thought Creighton looked like a born Sioux, especially admiring his craggy, hawk-featured face. Their name for him was Cetan Mani, literally, The-Hawk-That-Walks, or, as it subsequently became famous throughout the Sioux Nation, "Walking Hawk."

sleepy-eyed fellow officers. "What's five hundred Indians more or less?"

"Yes, Perez," agreed Colonel Clanton, "what about it? Hang it all, man, you didn't get us out of bed to tell us you'd found five hundred Indians." On his words, the office door opened soundlessly. Creighton, the other scout, slid inside the room to stand quietly against the wall.

"I allow ye didn't hear me," Perez answered the colonel, evenly. "I said 'Tashunka Witko.' If thet don't wake ye up, nothin' will."

"Oh, quit talking like a damn Indian Perez." Their enforced association had done nothing to diminish Stacey's dislike of the half-breed. "Who the hell is Tashunka Witko?"

"Yes," echoed Colonel Clanton, stiffly, "are we supposed to be excited?"

"I am," announced Perez, simply.

"Well?" The colonel's query soaked up a shade of the scout's seriousness.

"Tashunka Witko is the most dangerous Sioux livin'. Happen ye hear more about Red Cloud and Sittin' Bull, but they cain't tech Tashunka. Sittin' Bull's a great Injun. So's Red Cloud. They're real chiefs. *Wagh!* But when it comes to fightin', they both tooken their lessons from Tashunka. And they're takin' their orders from him, too. Ye kin stake yer hoss to thet. I've lived with him and I know him. And when he shows up it means jest one thing."

"What?" challenged Stacey, bluntly.

"War." Perez' one word was as flat as the look that followed it out into the room.

"Now, see here, Perez." Colonel Clanton's patient voice was still uninterested. "It's plain you're dead serious, but I'll be damned if I know what you're getting at." The rare use of the profanity did not escape Perez. "What in the world is so disturbing to you about this Tashunka Witko? I don't believe I've heard the name."

"No, nor have any of the rest of us," broke in Stacey, belligerently.

"Mebbe ye'd like thet name better in English!" The low-voiced interruption came from behind the group. The younger officers, not lacking in imagination to the extent their senior was, and made nervous by Perez' dark words, whirled jumpily. What they saw was the raw-boned civil scout, John Creighton, standing in the lamp shadows by the door, tall and dark as any Sioux.

71

"Damn you, Creighton!" Stacey's tones were angry with uneasiness. "I wish to hell you'd knock when you sneak in. You red-lovers are all alike, bellying around corners like so many goddam Indians."

"I'm waitin' to translate 'Tashunka Witko' fer ye," the scout reminded them, grinning his enjoyment of the situation. "Git a firm holt on yer hair, boys." The officers waited while Creighton ran his hard eyes over them. "Crazy Horse!" He jumped the words at them, deliberately, not being disappointed in the way they ducked them.

"You might as well have said 'Boo!' for all the silly damn dramatics," growled Stacey. "What are we supposed to do now, wet our pants? Do you think you're funny, Creighton?"

"No," the white scout's reply slipped into the warm room like an icicle, "and I don't think ye are, either. Ye're supposed to be a competent officer on duty in the hottest hostile spot on the map, and ye haven't got wits enough to add up Crazy Horse and five hundred Oglala fightin' men movin' across country in the guts of winter. It's like two-and-two, and the answer come out whut Pawnee said—war."

Before Stacey's fury could find words, Colonel Clanton stepped in. "Creighton, I think you'd better apologize. After all, Major Stacey is a senior officer and certainly a gentleman. I won't have you—"

"Sorry, Colonel," the scout came in, narrow-eyed, "I won't apologize and I won't serve under any sech officer as Stacey. I'm through."

Major Stacey's agreement spat with anger. "I'll say you're through, you impertinent goddam—"

"Shet him up, Colonel. I won't take his cussin', nor any man's." The big scout's hand slid down and back, its shadow hovering over the low-hanging butt of the Colt.

"Gentlemen! I'll remind both of you where you are!" Colonel Clanton's indignant words filled the dangerous pause. "The discussion's ended. I want Creighton and Perez to remain. For the rest of you 'good night' and quick about it." His final words crowded out the door behind the departing officers. "And I don't want any talk of Crazy Horse spreading around the garrison. Is that clear? Major Stacey, I'll want to see you as soon as I'm through with the scouts."

With the officers gone, the colonel turned at once to Creighton. "Do you agree with Perez on the gravity of his report?"

"Sure as hoss stinks. Crazy Horse is the top Sioux War Chief. Hell, he's *the* War Chief, and no argyments from nobody on it.

He's not movin' his village in wintertime jest fer the hell of it, either."

"It's a war village," said Perez. "No squaws along, no children, no old people."

"What do you propose doing?" Clanton asked both of them, getting his answer from the half-breed.

"Somebody's got to keep tailin' thet village. If thar's anythin' goin' on up thar in the Wolves, Crazy Horse'll lead us to it. Creighton has got hisse'f a private hunch thar's a big war camp up in thar sommers. I'd listen to thet hunch."

"How about it, Creighton? Do you want to go after that village? On up into the Wolves?" The colonel was decidedly lukewarm.

"I'm goin', all right, but not up into the Wolves. I'm through workin' at Will Farney and I allow ye know why."

"Don't be childish, Creighton. You're working for me. Just forget Stacey."

"I aim to. My outfit's packed and I'm pullin' out tonight."

"Well, I won't argue with you." Clanton was suddenly on his dignity. "I've been thinking you've been getting a little soft on the Indians lately. I'll have no man scouting on my rolls whom I suspect of thinking more of his red brothers than his white. Sergeant Simpson will draw your due pay. You can leave in twenty minutes." Creighton's face was as expressionless as a Cheyenne's. Watching him, Perez knew what was passing in his mind. If a man didn't spit on an Indian and call him a lousy, red bastard, right off that man was an Indian lover. On the frontier you were either for them or against them, when it came to Indians. The white side, the *Wasicun*, admitted no shades of color in between. Especially of the *Wasicun* Army was this thinking true. Every scout worth his meat-salt in the trade knew damn well that it was a matter of forty good Indians and ten bad ones, all the way down the line. The Army said, "In a pig's ass!" If there were fifty Indians there were fifty lousy, red bastards and that was that, with the "amen" delivered by the Reverend Doctor Spencer Carbine just as soon as he could see copper-colored hide between his sights.

John Creighton, returning Clanton's annoyed stare with one as long and cool as a Georgia julep, answered him at last, his slow, Southern voice letting the words out wide and soft. "If ye think I'm an Injun lover, Colonel, mebbe ye're right. But if ye think I'd go against my own color to he'p them, happen ye're full of hoss shit." The big white scout turned

73

and left the room before the high purple in Clanton's face could transform itself into syllables.

When the door had closed, the post commander controlled himself with an effort, passed his hand slowly over his forehead. When he spoke it was in weariness rather than irritation. "Let's sleep on it, Pawnee. I think the whole thing's a whisper in a whirlwind. I've got four hundred regulars inside the best stockade on the frontier. I can't see anything happening."

"Somebody ought to go on up, tonight," reiterated the half-breed. "I would but I bin out sixty hours, now."

"There's nobody else to go," Clanton informed him. "Bailey and O'Connor went up the Virginia City Road this afternoon —two squads of cavalry and a big supply train for the mines."

"God help them, they'll never git through," commented Perez, adding quietly, "I'll go back out in the mornin'."

"Well, all right. But you don't have to go back out, Pawnee. You scouts have all been around Indians so much you can't see any other color than red."

"Happen ye're right," Perez' final words managed to be ominous for all their softness. "I'm seein' red, right now. I said, months ago, thet the Sioux would hit ye with the first big snow. Thet snow's comin'. I smelled it on the wind, tonight. Mebbe twenty-four, forty-eight hours, but it's comin' and it's comin' big."

"A 'red blizzard,' eh, Perez?" Clanton's little laugh was patronizing.

"A red blizzard," echoed Perez, and went out of the room.

The night Pawnee Perez returned to Fort Farney with the news of Crazy Horse's big war village was the nineteenth of December. The next day dawned clear and bright with no cloud bigger than a pipe-puff in the sky. Clanton and Stacey were in fine spirits. In their respective ways, the one with ponderous good humor, the other with caustic sarcasm, both had chided Perez about his "blizzard," but by late afternoon the horizon to the north lay piled high with lumpy shoulders of lead-gray cloud. The wind dropped to a muttering whisper and an uneasy quiet lay over Fort Farney. By 5 P.M., as Sergeant Murdo Murphy put it, "A ring-nosed sow with the snortin' sniffles could have smelled snow with her snoot in six inches of swill."

To begin the day Clanton had ordered Perez to abandon his proposed scouting trip to hang a constant tail on Crazy

74

Horse's war pony and, instead, had ordered him to take a wood train out.

Hawk Creighton had been bulletined to go out with the wood detail, but with him gone the chancy job of guiding it had fallen to Perez.

There was no trouble, the half-breed getting the loaded wagons back to the fort about 4 P.M. He hadn't seen a moccasin track or a feather tip, hadn't heard an owl hoot or a fox bark, and was more certain than ever that the sullen blizzard building to the north held disaster for Fort Will Farney in its dirty, gray gut.

When he reported to Colonel Clanton, he repeated his blizzard hunch and the warning that went with it. "Colonel, I never heard so much quiet in my life. I didn't run over ary a pony track the livelong day."

"That's good," nodded the officer. "Precisely as I told you, Perez, there's nothing to worry about."

"Happen ye know Injuns," the scout demurred, "thar's plenty to worry about. Old Jim Bridger allus told me, 'When ye don't see 'em, thet's when they're thar,' and Old Jim writ the book about Injuns. They're out thar sommers"—a quick hand-wave to the north—"and, mister, I *know* they are."

Clanton missed the odd use of the "mister," but not the scout's intensity. "Well, Pawnee, you were right about the blizzard, by the look of that north sky," he admitted uneasily, "perhaps you're right about the hostiles. I'll have Stacey mount a double guard on the stockade and change the outposts on Signal and Humpback Hills every two hours. Will that satisfy you?"

"Better'n a buffler errer in the butt," grunted the scout, "but if I was ye, I'd—" His words were broken off by Major Stacey's sudden entrance.

"Bailey and O'Connor are back!" Stacey's color was high and getting higher. "Just came in the east gate. Black Shield and a big bunch of Minniconjou jumped them up north of Wolf Creek Crossing. They lost all the wagons. Lieutenant Wander and Sergeant Schofield killed, five troopers wounded. Bailey says the only reason they got away at all is that the Sioux stopped to fight over the stuff in the wagons."

"Well, good God, send them in here!" Clanton, for once aroused, was shouting. "Let's get the whole story. Hurry up, Stacey!"

"They're gone!" ejaculated the red-bearded officer.

"Grabbed fresh horses and lit out, south. Said Hawk Creighton and the half-breed were right all along. Claimed they were getting out while the getting was good."

"This is serious, Stacey." Clanton sank back in his desk chair. "For God's sake what are we going to do for scouts? Perez is the only one left!"

"What of it, Colonel?" Stacey's question leapt with eagerness. "We don't need a scout to find those Minniconjou. Let me take a column out and teach the goddam redbirds a lesson. Bailey said Black Shield followed them down but caught up with them too close to the fort to jump them again. Let me go out in the morning. It's the chance we've been waiting for!"

"How many troops do you want?"

"Two companies will be plenty!"

"Black Shield's a pretty salty-peckered chief," announced Perez, slowly. "I wouldn't figure him to have less'n three hunderd braves along."

"Well?" Stacey's challenge was quick with temper.

"Thet yer idee of good odds—four to one?"

"I've said so!"

"Me," said the scout, thoughtfully, "I wouldn't step out'n this fort to pee, with less'n a thousand men holdin' my hand."

"We can't let this attack go by, Perez," declared Clanton, flatly. "If the storm is still holding off in the morning, we're going out. You can have your two companies, Stacey. It's time we took off our gloves."

Stacey thanked his superior and departed to organize his command. No sooner had he gone than Sergeant Simpson stepped in, saluting. "Pardon me, Colonel. That scout, Hawk Creighton, he just came back to the fort. Wants to see you, sir. Says it's real important—"

"Ye kin relax, Simpson," grunted Creighton, coming in at the door, bumping roughly past the sergeant. Without benefit of giving Clanton time to get his open mouth shut, the white scout gave it to him brief and sweet. "I changed my mind when I left here, Colonel. Couldn't let well enough alone. Had to run out thet bunch of Pawnee's and mine about thet big war camp up above."

"Yes?"

"Wal, I found it. Fifty miles up the Tongue. About a thousand lodges. Thet means better'n two thousand warriors. Mostly Sioux, some Cheyenne, a few Arapahoe. I snuck in thar about an hour short of daylight. Tashunka Witko had jest come into camp and they were havin' a whale of a pow-wow.

It was still blacker'n the insides of a buck's gut, so I bellied in close enough to hear plenty. They're goin' to follow thet blizzard down onto the fort, Pawnee," the quick nod went to Perez. "Ye were right about thet."

"What do you suggest we do?" The fort commander's inherent lack of imagination was fading rapidly under the apparent respect of both the seasoned mountain scouts for Crazy Horse and his war camp in the Wolves. Colonel Travis Clanton was a slow man to grasp a tactical picture, but by no means blunderheaded-blind, like Stacey.

"Get ready fer a siege, thet's all. Whut else kin ye do?" Hawk Creighton shrugged the suggestion.

"Major Stacey wants to go out with a column in the morning," remembered Clanton, uneasily. "What about that?"

"Thet's nice," grinned Creighton. "They'll butcher him quicker'n a squaw kin gut a dog."

"I don't agree with you, there, Creighton!" The colonel's objection showed a little nettle. "You scouts are all Indian-jumpy. I think Stacey could break up the attack before it got well started."

"Ye mean ye're actually goin' to let thet fool go out?" The hulking frontiersman's words were unbelieving. "Right square in the face of whut I bin tellin' ye?"

"It all depends on the weather. We'll see. The thing to do now is get the fort ready for repelling this attack of yours just in case it materializes. You two men go get some sleep. You're all the scouts I have and if Stacey goes out in the morning, one of you will have to go with him."

"It won't be me," advised the tall white scout crooked-grinning the words, acidly.

Colonel Clanton didn't hear him, his own shouts for his sergeant filling the room. "Simpson. Ho, Simpson! Get the officer of the day in here."

"Yes, sir! Anything else, sir?"

"Yes. You might as well tell the rest of the officers to get in here, too. And tell them to hop it!"

"Yes, sir!" responded Simpson, beating his own answer out the door.

Perez and Hawk Creighton squatted along the wall of Clanton's office, smoking. Around them the normal evening quiet of the post began to break up as Hawk's report of the coming Indian assault spread throughout the garrison. Groups of enlisted men began clotting up on the parade yard west of Colonel Clanton's office. In a matter of minutes the officers had all reported in and the conference was under way. Over the fort a subdued hum began to grow, at first faint and indefinite, rapidly becoming positive and unmistakable—the whispering lisping gibberish of hundreds of frightened human tongues muttering in the dark.

As yet no official confirmation of Creighton's report had gone out from Clanton, no orders had been issued, no alert given. But the fort *knew*, and the fear of that knowing hung over it so heavy you could feel it pressing down like a thick, moist hand.

Quietly sucking their pipes in the shadows, watching the nervous officers approaching and entering the C.O.'s office, Perez and Creighton were discussing, of all things, the weather.

"When do ye figure she'll hit?" the big Southerner wanted to know.

Perez, studying the sky to the north, which even in that black night seemed to have a dirty color independent of the surrounding darkness, took his time in answering. "Along about noon to dark, tomorry."

"Closer to night, maybe, huh?"

"Yeah."

"Gonna be a big one."

"Big as a bull's ass," grunted the half-breed.

"Whut do ye aim to do, Pawnee?"

"Stick around," shrugged Perez. "How about ye?"

"Yeah, I'll stick, too. Ye figure thet damn fool will go out in the mornin'?"

"Sure. Don't ye?"

"Yeah, I reckon. Ye goin' out with him like Clanton asked ye, Pawnee?"

Perez considered this a minute, hunching down in his wolf coat as he answered, "What else? A man's got to stick by his color."

"Ye kin duck out like Bailey and O'Connor. Nobody'd blame ye. By God, they're white and they didn't worry any about cuttin' their sticks. Besides, everybody knows Stacey's rid yer hump plumb raw around here."

"He's rid ye, too."

"Yeah," the white scout's words were pointed, "but not with the same spurs, Pawnee. I allow ye gather where I'm holdin' my sights."

78

"Yeah, I know. Ye're the only one thet's treated me like I was white."

"Ye're white. What the hell, ye look white." Hawk Creighton's statement was simple, without guile.

"My father was white," said Perez, and the two fell silent. After some minutes, Hawk knocked out his pipe. "Ye figure the hostiles will get into the stockade?"

"Likely not. If Stacey says inside."

"They'll go fer a try at baitin' him out, ye figure?"

"Sure," Perez nodded. "Don't ye?"

"Yeah, I allow so. What time is it?"

"About twelve."

"Conference ought to be breakin' up any minute," offered Creighton.

"Comin' out right now," grunted the black-bearded breed. "Thar's Benson and Drummond."

"And Stacey," added his companion. "Lookit the grin on him, will ye? Thet means he's got his way about tomorrow."

"It's a dead man's grin, if he did." Perez flashed a half-snarl of his white teeth.

"Reckon so," was all Hawk Creighton said.

The twenty-first dawned as sparkling-clear as the day preceding it, but it was frost-bitter cold. The crouching cloud to the north seemed not to have shifted its ominous bulk an inch. There could be no doubt, now, that Wasiya, the Winter Giant, was squatting up there back of the Wolves. It was equally obvious that the lead-gutted old devil was waiting for something. But for what? Down at Fort Will Farney the weather was as bright as a fresh-minted penny: no wind, no clouds, no worry.

It was cold, though—colder than the hubs of hell with the axles frozen.

Pawnee Perez stood outside Colonel Clanton's office, his hunched shoulders burrowing into the deep fur of the wolfskin hunting coat. The jutting black beard was already ice-tipped with the condensed moisture of his breathing. As he waited, a similarly fur-clad figure came slouching across the parade yard.

"Mornin', Pawnee. Nice day."

"Fer caribou, mebbe." The half-breed's short answer was garnished with the flash of his rare smile.

"Great day for seein' Injuns," Creighton continued. "A man

79

kin peel his eye clear past the Powder. Hell, it's runnin' too quiet around here. Me, I got me an urge to git some of the red sons."

"I reckon ye won't be disappointed."

"Likely ye're right." The white scout's voice sobered. "Whut do ye make of the weather, now?"

"Same like I said last night. She'll hit along late this afternoon."

"Me, I don't think so, no more," observed Creighton. "Old Wasiya appears to have sucked in his gut a mite. Looks to me like he's drawin' back sommat."

"Gittin' set to jump," grunted Perez.

"Might be ye're right. Stacey in there, now?" Creighton noded toward Clanton's door.

"Nope. Ain't showed yit."

"Speak of the devil—" his companion echoed, throwing his glance across the parade yard.

Major Stacey hurried up, brushing past the scouts to enter the colonel's office without a word. Creighton and Perez grinned at each other. "He's a cute one," opined the tall, white scout.

"Cuter then a heifer's tits in a bull's eye," agreed his swarthy comrade.

"Whut do ye think they'll do? Ye reckon Clanton will still let little red-beard go out chasin' Black Shield?"

"Dunno," Perez muttered, doubtfully. "The Old Boy's usually right cautious. He ain't bright but he ain't no bugle-blowin' hero like Stacey. He's had hisse'f a night to sleep on it. I allow he may have switched his mind some."

"I allow ye're right," Hawk nodded, thoughtfully, as the doors of Clanton's office opened. "Here comes God's gift to the cavalry, now. And get yerse'f a travois-load of thet face. The Old Boy's told him he cain't go out and play this mornin' and Junior's sore as a caked tit." As Stacey stomped past them, the big scout cooed innocently, "Good mornin', little man!"

"Kiss my ass!" snapped the officer, red-faced, his quick stride continuing unbroken.

"Thar's Simpson wavin' us to come in." Perez nodded to his companion. "Let's go."

"Right behind ye. *Hopo! Hookahey!*" grinned the big scout, following the half-breed toward the office. "I do hope the colonel's hind end ain't as puckered as his friend's this mornin'."

As expected, Colonel Clanton informed them he had advised Stacey to hold off on the planned excursion outside the fort. "I anticipate no real trouble, mind you, but I respect your opinions. At the same time I've instructed Major Stacey to get his troops ready in case the picture should change. If any of the hostiles show up outside, we're going after them. I'll go along with you two on its not being wise for us to go out beyond range of the fort looking for trouble, but damn it all, if those Indians come around here begging for a volley, they're going to get one!" The scouts looked at one another, saying nothing, and Clanton continued.

"Stacey seems to think he can handle the situation with his cavalry. Of course, should he go out, I'll insist on some infantry support. About six squads, I think." Again the scouts said nothing, and the post commander finished off, addressing Perez.

"As to scouts, Stacey won't have Creighton and he doesn't want you, Pawnee. But it was agreed that you would go with him in case of any punitive action. How about it, Perez? Will you go? And before you answer I must warn you, or better, remind you, that you are an enrolled Army scout. That makes your position a bit different than Creighton's. As a civilian, simply on our payroll, he exercises a certain freedom of movement not quite available to you. I, uh—"

"Ye kin leave off the bugle blowin', Colonel." Perez' grin was a grin only by virtue of a flicking grimace of the wide mouth. The hard stare of the slant, black eyes failed to keep the quick expression even momentary company. "I'll go with Stacey." The hunched shoulders shrugged the statement. "If he's brain-struck enough to think he kin whup two thousand Sioux with less'n a full troop of Pony Soldiers, I allow I'm jest crazy enough to tag along and watch him try it."

"Good!" Colonel Clanton stood up. "You stick around, too, Creighton. If anything breaks I'll work you in on it, some way."

"I imagine," grunted the big scout, his eyes as black and expressionless as the half-breed's.

Outside, the tall white man drew a deep breath, exhaling slowly. "Whew! Well, thet's a relief. Now, all we got to worry about is the cussed Sioux sendin' in a bait party."

A dozen scattered rifle shots from the north stockade punctuated his statement. Both scouts whipped around in their tracks to stand like startled elk, heads up and into the wind, eyes narrowed, ears straining.

The dry crackling of the rifles continued atop the wall,

the answering lead from outside the fort whanging and ricocheting off the stockade's top logs.

"Ye kin start worryin', Hawk." The half-breed's dark head made a quick-darting nod northward. "Thar's yer bait party!"

The first shots were still echoing as Perez and Hawk Creighton raced for the north wall. Behind them, as they scrambled up the ladder to the catwalk atop the stockade, the fort was coming sharp awake.

Brass-lunged noncoms were bellowing a confusion of orders, troopers were tumbling from barracks partly armed, half asleep, completely rattled. Down by the main gate Captain Howell, Stacey's second, and the officer who'd been new to Perez in the first conference following his return from scouting Crazy Horse, was trying to marshal the detail Stacey had ordered formed up. Colonel Clanton was coming from his office in a puffing run, behind him, the chop-running figure of Major Phil Stacey.

"Whut do ye make of it, Pawnee," Hawk asked Perez, the two of them peering intently through the rifle slits.

"Hell, it's a bait party, no question. Seems to be jest the ten of them. And look how they've split thet ten up. Two each of Oglala, Hunkpapa, Minniconjou, Cheyenne and Arapahoe. Thet's no accident."

"Cripes, no! They probably sat up half the night arguin' who would git the honor of bein' in the bait party."

"Wal, sure," Perez nodded. "Thet'd give them the best chancet of gittin' the first *coups*."

"I reckon," Creighton muttered. "The crazy devils'll do anythin' to have the honor of swattin' the enemy first, won't they?"

"Yeah."

"Whut do ye make out'n this bait, Pawnee?"

"It fer sure means the main bunch is layed up for a ambush. They're hopin' to git some of the Eagle Chief's soldiers to come out and go to chasin' them."

"Thet's fer sure," agreed the white scout. "Lookit the nutty sons ridin' around out there! They don't give a good goddam fer all the leads thet's bein' slung their way."

"They got more brass then a bronze monkey's butt when they're really up to somethin'." Perez' words were terse. "I hope to Christ Colonel Clanton ain't goin' to fall fer thet come-on."

"Hey, Pawnee!" The half-breed's fellow watcher was suddenly excited. "Do ye see whut I see? Way over there on Humpback Hill. Jest below thet cedar clump thet sticks up like a topknot." Perez' searching gaze followed his companion's. "Thet's him, ain't it?" The white scout's question was tense.

"It's him," the half-breed muttered. "I could tell thet red ramrod ten miles off, let alone three. Looks like he'd been starched stiff, then glued on to stay."

"Make out anybody with him? Must be four or five of them."

"Cain't be sure about the riders from this distance, exceptin' Tashunka, like I said. But from the hosses I'd say, let's see . . . Thet's Red Cloud's paint stud—Dull Knife's appaloosie—White Bull's sockfoot sorrel. I don't recollect thet other pony but I'd guess it was American Horse sittin' him. He usually rides a black like thet and wears one of them seven-foot war-bonnets."

"*Aii-eee!*" Creighton grimaced. "They got their heavy guns with them today."

"Yeah," Perez grunted, "and hyar comes ours!" His gesture indicated Colonel Clanton and Major Stacey coming toward them along the catwalk.

"Well, boys," the colonel's query was brisk, "what do you make of this?"

"Yes!" Stacey echoed him, triumphantly. "What *do* you think of this, boys? Where's your two thousand warriors, Creighton?"

"Waitin' fer ye to come prancin' and brayin' out of the fort with yer Pony Soldiers," the scout answered, acidly.

"You think those are decoys out there?" Colonel Clanton, as usual, was patiently serious.

"Thar ain't no question," Perez answered for both scouts. "The main bunch is out thar. We jest seen Crazy Horse and three, four other big chiefs over on Humpback Hill."

"I don't see anybody over there on Humpback." This from Stacey. "And besides, don't be ridiculous! That's our second signal station over on that hill."

"Well, now ye know why ye didn't get any signal from thet station," growled Hawk Creighton, searching the hillside again, seeing that the Indians had indeed disappeared.

"No, and ye never will," added Perez, quietly. "Them boys have lost their hair. How about the other station, Colonel? The one on Signal Hill?"

83

"Simpson brought me a helio from them just now. They flashed 'Many Indians' five times, then quit."

"They're gone, too," said Perez, simply.

"The hell you say!" contradicted Stacey, the irrepressible. "They probably abandoned post. They'll show up any minute, now."

"Well," Colonel Clanton's interruption hit the scouts like a knife in the ribs, "in any event, we've got that hay train out there, and—"

"Ye've whut?" Perez literally shouted.

"A hay train, four wagons," Colonel Clanton countered stiffly, taken aback by the half-breed's slit-eyed vehemence. "Sergeant Murphy and sixteen men. Went out at four this morning. They should have been back by now. We needed that hay"—the colonel spoke defensively now, knowing by Perez' utterly contemptuous sneer, and Hawk Creighton's black-lined scowl, that he'd erred, tragically—"and Major Stacey figured we could get it in before the Sioux showed up. From Creighton's report, Stacey figured the Sioux couldn't possibly get down here before noon, at the earliest."

"Whut does he figure now?" Perez threw his knife-glance into the junior officer, with the question.

"I still figure I'm right!" snapped Stacey, defiantly. "If the hay wagons have been jumped, it's by a band of scouts or by that scoundrel, Black Shield. That main body of hostiles Creighton reported couldn't possibly have gotten down here yet. Providing," Stacey's sneer was a triumph of delicacy, "they're coming at all."

"And I told ye they'd get down here before daylight!" The big white scout's tones were flat with anger. "Thet was *my* report, damn ye."

"And I say not before noon, damn *you!*" Stacey was shouting. "We haven't heard a shot from up there. That hay meadow is only six miles out. We could hear any firing up there!"

As if to document the accuracy of the officer's angry observation, a faint popping of musket fire carried down to the fort on the freshening north wind. In a momentary lull in the nearer firing of the hostile decoys outside the stockade, the more distant shots rode in clearly.

"We thank ye, Sergeant Murphy," drawled Hawk Creighton sarcastically, tipping his foxskin cap graciously in the direction of the musket fire. "Ye've shown us thet Major Stacey at least knows how far ye kin hear a musketshot when the wind's jest so."

"Thet's from over west of Peyo Crick," barked Perez, ignoring his companion's irony, quickly checking the sounds of the shots. "Is thet hay outfit workin' in Bay Hoss Meadow?"

"Yes"—this, nervously, from Clanton. "Isn't that right, Stacey?"

"Yes, sir. Bay Horse Meadow. And with your permission, Colonel, I'll go out after them, right now!"

"Naturally, man! We've got to bring them in. Get a move on, Stacey. And, Stacey, take along six squads of infantry!"

"We can't spare them from the fort, sir," the major's statement crackled with inspired decision, "foot soldiers would slow us down, and, by the Lord, sir, I don't need them!"

At this point Perez, racking his mind for an out to save the men about to be committed to this irresponsible command, glanced down to see the new captain, Howell, sitting his horse at the head of the waiting mounted troop, below. Perez didn't know Howell but he allowed he knew men. A man could easy see the difference between the unknown officer and Stacey. The captain looked as cool as a brook trout under a willow root.

"Colonel," the breed's voice lost none of its intestines through its purring softness, "why not let Captain Howell go out with the mounted relief? Hawk kin take them. Then I kin foller with Major Stacey and the six squads of infantry. Thet way we kin at least keep the whole relief detail from gittin' cut off."

Colonel Clanton opened his mouth to agree with the half-breed's suggestion, but Stacey struck into the opening, deft as a lance-jab. The red-bearded cavalryman's mind was as quick as it was quirky. "A damn good idea, Perez!" he exclaimed, heartily. "But Howell's too good a man on defense. I'm not worth a cent on this cooped-up fort fighting. Had all my experience with open movements. You know, cavalry stuff. But whatever the colonel says, of course!" Too many years the Regular Army man, Major Phil Stacey, not to know the optimum moment for the neat wafting of a posterior osculation, rankward.

"Stacey's right!" The fort commander succumbed to the dangerous contagion of his junior's beautiful confidence. "I need Howell here. Go ahead, Phil, but for God's sake be careful! Your orders are to go out and bring that hay train in,

85

and *nothing* else. I agree with the scouts that those Indians out there beyond the stockade are decoys. Pay no attention to them. And whatever happens, don't go past Eagle Point on the main road. Under *no* circumstances are you to proceed past Eagle Point, down Squaw Pine Ridge. Is that absolutely clear?"

"Yes, sir!" Stacey's eyes were snapping, wildly.

"Perez will go with you, and, Stacey," here the C.O.'s voice labored with weight, "under all conditions you are to respect his opinions. I want that understood. We're in trouble here, now, without adding any slap-dash Indian chasing."

"All right, Perez!" In the moment of Major Stacey's coming triumph, even the despised half-breed was eagerly accepted. "Let's go!"

Hawk Creighton had stood by, wordless, throughout this last exchange. Now, his voice went sharply to Colonel Clanton. "Colonel, let me go with them. I cain't do anythin' here. I'm a scout."

Stacey was already swinging to the ground below, but Perez caught the remark, stepping quickly back toward his fellow scout. The half-breed's eyes were burning like six-hour coals, his lean face, dark-flushed. In Pawnee Perez "that feeling" was coming up. The wind of the hunt was in his nostrils, bringing the death-stink of Yunke-lo with it. When he spoke, the words came in the barking gutturals of the High Plains Sioux.

"No!" His slit-eyed stare riveted the white scout. "This hyar's my war party. Ye stay hyar. Thet crazy Oak Leaf fool," jerking a thumb toward Stacey, "is ridin' a dead man's pony. Somebody's got to stay hyar whut kin bring a support party out to us fast. Thet's ye, Hawk!" His long, brown finger stabbed suddenly at Creighton.

Before either the colonel or Creighton could answer, Perez had dropped off the catwalk, twelve feet to the ground below, was running, high-shouldered and unbelievably swift, toward his waiting dun gelding.

"I'll be damned if he isn't a strange duck," stammered the officer. "Never saw such a man."

"Duck? Man? Hell!" The white scout's fascinated gaze followed the hunched figure of the running breed. "Did ye ketch thet look he give me? And the way his voice went to growlin' along with it? And do ye see the lopin' way he runs? Ever see a *man* run thet way?"

"Can't say that I have," the colonel's answer was brief, distracted.

"He's a wolf." Hawk Creighton's words came as quiet as they did certain.

Fifty infantry, thirty horse, three officers, one Army scout; quickly they went, splashing across the ice-rimmed shallows of Spruce Creek, forging up the narrow Virginia City Road, the foot soldiers at a swinging double, the cavalry at a jingling trot.

With the infantry strode stolid Captain ·Robert Benson, thinking of his wife and three-months-old daughter, behind him in the precarious shelter of Fort Will Farney. And with Benson, youthful Second Lieutenant Barrett Drummond, remembering his pretty bride fluttering her gay kerchief after him from the north stockade gate.

With the horse troop, square-faced Major Phil Stacey, thinking of nothing but teaching the Sioux a bloody lesson, remembering nothing but his own willful determination to be a hero.

Well, a lesson was taught that day and it was a bloody one: a hero was made, but he was a dead one.

Stacey was barely out of sight of the fort before disobeying his first order. Instead of ignoring the decoys, he pressed hard after them.

Perez at once reminded him of Clanton's express orders forbidding just this tactic, being thanked for his concern by a cheerfully spleenful suggestion that he return to the fort as fast as his yellow-bellied horse could carry him. The half-breed's wide mouth clamped into a thin slash above the sooty beard. His narrow face seemed frozen by more than the rising wind as he answered, softly, "Major Stacey, if ye go past Eagle Point down Squaw Pine Ridge, I quit."

"I know the orders, Perez." The officer was too excited to consider seriously the scout's warning. "You stick to scouting, I'll run the troops."

The half-breed hadn't answered, merely slouching lower in his saddle, hunching his narrow head, swinging his restless gaze more nervously than ever.

As the troops approached the forbidden Squaw Pine Ridge, the decoys became unaccountably bolder, riding back in crazy dashes at the leading group of Pony Soldiers, scarcely firing their own rifles, their purpose clearly to excite and draw out.

Stacey played obediently to their lead, urging his mounted command forward, widening the gap between it and the following foot soldiers. Perez took sudden note of three things: all firing from Bay Horse Meadow had ceased; the sky overhead, blue when the troops left the fort, had gone sullenly gray; the trail was narrowing dangerously.

At this point, the track of the Virginia City Road ran along the spine of a high, bare ridge, the sides of which pitched their ice-patched slopes downward at dizzy angles. Ahead, half a mile, lay Eagle Point, the beginning of the sharp downdrop of Squaw Pine Ridge. Perez, thinking now of the way Peyo Creek forked the bottom of that ridge, kneed his pony in alongside Stacey's.

"Squaw Pine is jest ahead—" he began, Stacey cutting him short.

"Let's worry about that when we get there." The officer's tones were as gay as a pheasant hunter's with a fat covey under his feet and plenty of shells in his belt. Perez disregarded the interruption.

"—The ridge pitches down, steep, to Peyo Crick Flats. Thar's heavy timber jest beyond. I figure the main bunch will be in thet timber and in the gullies runnin' up both flanks of the ridge."

"Still looking for the lethal ambush, eh, Perez?" Stacey was almost friendly in his exuberance. "Well, I don't give a damn what you figure, my boy! I'm out here to remind your red brothers they can't knock over our supply trains and shoot up our work details. They've been giving us hell for three months and now, by God, they're going to get it back!"

Again Perez ignored him. "Murphy's quit firin'. Thet means he's either wiped out or they've left him to come over and help Crazy Horse spring the *wickmunke* on ye. In the first case we cain't he'p him none, and in the second he's probably already on his way back to the fort. In either case we ain't goin' to be of no he'p to him by goin' ahaid now."

"You're not only an Indian, Perez," Stacey actually laughed, "you're getting to be a squaw!"

For the third time, the scout disregarded the officer's remarks. "The blizzard is movin' in on us. An hour from now ye won't be able to see the trail, let alone the hostiles."

At the moment, not even the half-breed had any idea of the gruesome accuracy of his statement. An hour from then Major Phil Stacey wasn't seeing anything—Indians, trail, sky, snow, anything. His eyes were staring, wide-open, but they weren't seeing a thing; an optical peculiarity most common to the vision of dead men.

For the nonce, though, Major Stacey's health was as high as his spirits. As he answered the scowling half-breed, open sky showed ahead in the trail, marking the downward plunge of Squaw Pine Ridge.

Silhouetted against that patch of gray, the hostiles checked their rearing horses, shaking their feather lances, the half-dozen who possessed them firing their muskets into the air, the whole pack of them screaming the choicest Sioux and Cheyenne invective into the buffeting wind. Obligingly, that chill carrier whipped the savage insults back along the wind-swept ridge to the frozen ears of the following troops.

Stacey laughed aloud, his voice shaking with that eagerness that gets into a hound's belling when he's running hot-smell close on a wolf's track, and just before the wolf turns and rips his bawling throat from leather to leather. "There's your Eagle Point, Perez! What do you say, now? Still want to go home to the colonel?"

But Perez wasn't listening to the officer. Ahead, the decoys had turned and plunged off the skyline, down the pitching decline of Squaw Pine Ridge. One of their number, a huge Oglala brave riding a flashing bay and white pinto, hesitated, cupping his right hand to direct a last, hoarse challenge. The words came bucketing back to the troops, the deep Sioux gutturals carrying boomingly.

"*Ho, Sunke Wakan Manoan! Hehaha akicita tela opawinge wancel H'g'un! H'g'un!*"

"What the hell is the bastard saying?" Stacey grinned, happily.

"Thet was Sunke Sha, Red Dog the Oglala. We're old friends. I shot his brother in a wagon scrape up the Road last summer. 'Pears he remembers it," mutttered Perez, grimly. "He called me by their name for me, The Pony Stealer. Said the medicine man had promised them a hunderd dead white soldiers. Red Dog hoped Pony Stealer would be among the hunderd, and thet his heart was good."

Wheeling in his saddle, Major Stacey shouted back to his infantry. "Benson! Drummond! Close up. Come on, hurry!" By this time his own group had reached Eagle Point, checking there for Benson and Drummond to come up.

Squaw Pine Ridge ran in a thirty-degree decline, a distance

of perhaps six hundred yards, to the flats of Peyo Creek. Riding these flats, now, the Indian decoys raced and spun their ponies.

Shortly, Benson and Drummond joined Stacey, and the three officers, with Perez, studied the scene below.

"Perez thinks there's two thousand hostiles hidden in that timber and the gullies flanking this ridge." Stacey was flushed, talking excitedly. "He thinks they're laying for us to come down there. Personally," the words rattled out in the stillness, "I think there's no more than three hundred of them in any event, probably the same band that jumped our supply train yesterday—Black Shield's outfit." The major looked at his juniors, challengingly. "What do you think?"

Benson's answer was fast and honest, bristling with nerves. "Dammit, I don't know, Phil. I'm scared as hell for some reason."

Young Drummond was neither confused nor intimidated, being easily Stacey's equal for dash and bright judgment. "By God, I think you're right, Major! And if that is Black Shield's gang down there," here the youngster's voice went properly dramatic, "I want a crack at them. I went through the Academy with George Wander!"

Perez said nothing, his half-Pawnee mind telling him what an idiot this young *Wasicun* was, assuring him at the same time that Stacey wouldn't think of letting any dribble-nosed shavetail outgo him at being an utter damn fool. The scout's dour *Shacun* reasoning was instantly borne out.

"Yes, by heaven!" Stacey got into the Selfless Act with both booted feet. "Schofield was the best company sergeant a man ever had. I mean to get my pound of flesh for him, too. And, by God, it'll be *red* flesh!"

Perez' words dropped onto the end of Stacey's noble pronouncement like the slotted door of a box trap. "I won't go down with ye. I heered yer orders from Colonel Clanton even if these hyar boys didn't. I'm in my rights to quit right hyar. And, mister, I'm quittin'."

"You scum-bellied half-breed bastard!" The commanding officer's bitterness was broken into by a thundering shout from below. All eyes were immediately focused on Peyo Creek Flats.

Out of the timber flanking the level meadow charged three hundred mounted braves, men and horses daubed, decked and smeared with vermilion, ocher, cobalt, eagle feathers, heron plumes, dyed hair tassels, scalp-locks, buffalo horns, bear

90

claws, beads, quills, copper and silver ornaments, pennoned lances and gaudy blankets: the full, wild treatment of the paganly beautiful Sioux war dress.

At the banks of the creek the charge halted, the Indian horsemen pulling their mounts back to leave the figure of a lone chief standing out against their painted ranks.

On the ridge above, Perez cursed viciously. The one thing he hadn't anticipated! Once again, the fox-minded Red Cloud had outsharped his adopted Pawnee son. The identity of that chief, below, shot the last chance of stopping Stacey square between the eyes. His appearance at that moment was a master stroke of red planning. The half-breed made an inner bow to the fertile brains of Makhpiya Luta and Tashunka Witko, even as he tightened his knees on Sosi's ribs preparatory to wheeling the gelding for Fort Will Farney.

The following action went precisely as Perez knew it must.

"Who's that chief?" Stacey's barked question rapped out in the cold, still air.

"Black Shield," said Perez, heavy-voiced.

"Black Shield!" The commander's shout let one and all know that he, Stacey, stood vindicated, the lowly half-breed scout discredited. "You hear that, boys? Just what I said! There's the red son of a bitch who got our train and there's our Indians with him—*just three hundred of them!* Let's get on down there!"

Perez tried one last, desperate interruption. "Major, me and Hawk Creighton seen Red Cloud and Crazy Hoss this mornin'. Don't go down thar. Fer Christ's sake, don't do it. They're waitin' fer ye, baitin' ye with Black Shield. Cain't ye see thet? Captain Benson"—here, seeing from the bleak look on Stacey's face that the senior officer's ears were covered, the scout wheeled on Benson—"I swear Stacey's jumpin' his orders. Don't ye foller him down thar. Colonel Clanton'll back ye up, Captain. I heerd him order Stacey not under no circumstances to go down Squaw Pine Ridge. Ye've got a wife and baby back thar in the fort. Fer the sakes of them and all the other women and kids back thar, I'm—"

Stacey's voice, furious with tension, cut in viciously. "Shut your dirty mouth, Perez! One more word and you'll get this Colt in your belly. I can see Black Shield and three hundred braves. And I can see you're the same goddamn treacherous breed I always said you were. Now, cut your stick, Indian, and cut it fast. We're going down there and God help your lousy soul when I get back to Fort Will Farney!"

"God help yers," said Perez, evenly. "Ye'll never git back."

But Stacey was gone, shouting to his troops, starting them down the long decline. The Pawnee scout pulled his horse aside, to let them past. Youthful Captain Benson stepped after him, stood at his stirrup, talked quietly up to him. "Perez, tell Mrs. Benson how it was here. Tell her I said I loved her more than anything in the world. Ask her to kiss the baby for me." The frog-belly gray of the fear in the youth's face made the half-breed's stomach pull in and half turn. For some reason he put his hand down to the boy as he answered him, and the young officer took it like a child seizing his father's hand for help across a dangerous place.

"I'll tell her, Captain. Good luck. Ye might make it, boy. I bin wrong afore."

The youngster looked away from Perez, giving his hand a last wring. The scout didn't have to see his eyes. A man could feel the tears in that boy all the way through his fingertips. "Good-by, Perez," he said, before his voice choked and he jerked his clean, white hand from the half-breed's sinewy, dark paw, to go stumbling hurriedly after his command.

Perez sat his gelding, watching the white-faced troopers go over the lip of the ridge. Some of them looked at him curiously, a few waved, hesitantly, half smiling.

The scout returned the gestures without the smiles. These were brave, frightened men; fathers, husbands, sons; going, unquestioningly, out on the long trail. As they went, Perez honored them. And felt the bitter sorrow rise up inside of him for them. It was not the first, nor would it be the last, time that the brave had died under the orders of the vain.

Lieutenant Drummond, ranging the flank of his infantry troop, the last man over the edge, urged them to greater speed, cheerily calling out, "Come on, boys! Snap to it. We don't want them to get away!"

"They won't," Perez muttered, half aloud. "They'll wait fer ye."

With the words, he jerked Sosi hard around, pointing him back along the Virginia City Road. The little gelding jumped as the heels of the buffalo-hock boots hammered into his ribs. Seconds after the last of Drummond's men slid over the crest of Squaw Pine Ridge, the buckskin pony was belly-skimming the snow crust back toward Fort Will Farney.

Behind Perez, in the bottom gullies, along both frozen flanks of Squaw Pine Ridge, the Sioux were living out the letter of

92

the scout's last warning—they were waiting for Major Stacey and his "hundred white soldiers."

To the east crouched Makhpiya Luta, Red Cloud, with seven hundred mixed Cheyenne and Sioux; to the west, Tashunka Witko, with eight hundred Oglala and Hunkpapa Sioux. On the north, from the creek flats, Black Shield and his three hundred Minniconjou fired back at the advancing Pony Soldiers and Walk-a-Heaps.

Presently, the last group of infantry were past the halfway mark down the ridge. In the brush-choked gully on the west, Crazy Horse looked at High-Hump-Back and Man-Afraid-of-His-Horses. They nodded back, flint-eyed. "*Hopo!*" said Crazy Horse. "Let's go!"

In the timber butting the east flank of the ridge, Red Cloud turned to Dull Knife and Little Wolf. "Are your hearts brave?"

"We are ready. Our hearts are brave."

"*Hookahey!*" boomed Red Cloud. "Let's go!"

Stacey's eighty men heard the breaking drum of six thousand pony hoofs. They drew back, bunched and crowding, huddling down on the bare, icy spine of the ridge, a pitiful handful of confused white sheep, the cry of the Sioux wolf echoing terrifyingly in their startled ears.

Perez rode only a short way back along the Virginia City Road before putting Sosi down the steep sides of the hogback ridge. No use making it any easier for the Sioux than it had to be. Get down off the ridge and travel the gully bottoms—that was the only way.

He had not covered half the distance to the fort when a switch in the wind brought him the rhythm of galloping hoofs. He threw Sosi off the trail, forcing the little horse into a heavy spruce growth. Wrapping the gelding's nose, he waited, black eyes scanning the gully southward, right hand balancing the long Colt, lightly. Whoever it was riding this backtrail rode alone. The half-breed grinned. Some Sioux or Cheyenne lodge would be mourning tonight.

The figure which shortly came galloping up the gully was no Indian, however. Perez kicked Sosi back out onto the trail, the other rider sliding his gaunt bay to a snow-showering stop.

"Howdy, Pawnee. Whut the hell's the shootin' about?"

"Stacey's in a *wickmunke*, Hawk. I rode out on him when he went down Squaw Pine Ridge. Black Shield was teasin' him down by showin' hisse'f and three hundred Minniconjou on the creek flats. Stacey figured thet's all the hostiles thar

93

were, and down he went. I hit out before the shootin' started, but I know Tashunka and Makhpiya got him in a box he ain't never goin' to get out'n. Ye goin' on up?"

As the half-breed had talked, he'd seen Hawk Creighton's face stiffening up, knew damn well it wasn't ice in the wind that was doing the stiffening. The white scout's answer, though, gave no hint of what was making tracks behind his glittering eyes. "Yeah. Clanton heard the firin' and sent me out ahead of the relief. Captain Tendrake and fifty men are followin'."

"Hawk, ye'd best stay away from up thar." Perez was showing his Pawnee blood, growling his words in the prairie guttural. "It's no use. They got Stacey and they'll get ye."

"I'm goin'," said the white scout. "But ye'd best stay away from the fort. After leavin' yer troops like thet, ye know whut to expect from Clanton and his boys."

"Ye ain't lookin' at no hero, Hawk. This hyar's jest a job to me."

"Hell, I know thet!" snapped the other. "But Clanton'll figure ye deserted after the thing started, mebbe even hang the blame of the ambush on ye. It's been done before, ye know. Swing around Farney, Pawnee, and keep ridin'. Keep ridin' a fur piece."

"Go on back," the black-bearded breed's warning was harsh. "I'm goin' to warn Tendrake back, too. Thar's nothin' up thar fer him to relieve. Then I'm goin' on into the fort. Them fools has got to be warned and I aim to warn them. I had a white father, Hawk. Ye'll remember thet."

"So long." Creighton's eyes were suddenly carbon-hard. "I'm ridin' north."

"Ye're a fool," Perez said, and swung Sosi past his companion's mount, turning the little gelding southward and kicking him into a high lope.

The white scout watched the breed for a moment, then turned his own mount to ride north. In five seconds his figure was just a shadow; in ten it had disappeared completely.

The white door the thickening snows shut behind John Creighton was never opened. His body was never found, nor was his horse. The official records of Fort Will Farney list him as a heroic casualty of the Stacey Massacre. Indian legend tells another tale, but that Powder River country is full of legends and you can't believe any of them.

Fifteen minutes after leaving Creighton, Perez rode into

the head of Tendrake's relief column. Repeating his story, he got the expected reception of it.

"Good God, Perez! How could you leave them? That's desertion, pure and simple. You're on the Army rolls, an enlisted scout. Clanton will hang you."

"I'm not enlisted," snapped the half-breed. "I never took them stripes Clanton offered me."

"You're a Regular Army scout, Perez. You'll be tried that way. And Colonel Clanton will hang you!"

"Wal, I aim to give him the chancet!" The Pawnee's white teeth slashed at the words. "And if ye'd admire to watch my feet kickin', ye'd best turn around and come home with me. Take my advice, Captain. Don't go down Squaw Pine Ridge, whatever ye do. Go on up, if ye insist, and mebbe if ye stay up on top of the Road, they won't come up after ye. Least-ways thet's yer only chancet if ye go on up. Stay up on top. Me, I wouldn't stick one inch of my worst enemy's pecker past Eagle Point fer less'n half int'rest in Sutter's Gold Mine."

"Obviously, you wouldn't risk your own neck, Perez. Get out of the way."

"Captain, don't go up thar. It's no use. They're all gone. Turn yer men around and haid back to the fort with me. We kin make it easy if we cut and run fer it."

"Perez, I wouldn't follow you three feet to keep from step-ping off the hot edge of hell. I'm going up. And as far as you heading back for the fort, that's absurd. Get out of the way!"

The half-breed nodded, pulling Sosi off the trail, slouched in his stirrups to watch the frightened men slog by.

The last the scout saw of Tendrake's command, it was going at a dogtrot up the Virginia City Road, the men leaning into the whipping wind, their column ragged and continually broken by the stumbling and falling of the soldiers in the treacherous footing of the ridgeback.

When Perez hammered on the north stockade gates it was 2 P.M., and as fish-belly gray as late twilight. The snow, al-ready beginning to pile in low-driving waves against the bottom logs of the fortress walls, was belching out of the mouth of a vomiting gale. The noise of the building storm was such by this time that no sound of firing to the north could be heard—if indeed there was any to hear.

Colonel Clanton listened to the half-breed's story in silence.

When it was done, his statement was typically heavy, characteristically open. "I've tried hard to like you, Pawnee, and I believe you will admit I've been more than fair with you. I've tried to think of you as a fellow white man, and to treat you like one."

"Ye have," nodded the half-breed, shortly. "Ye and Hawk Creighton, alone."

Clanton ignored his agreement, plodded on as a man with an ox's mind will, seeing the wagon ruts of his own thinking ahead, not looking for any other tracks. "But in this case I can't help you, man. You must know what the command here will think of your action. You will be accused of arrant cowardice as a matter of course. Further than that, there will be more than a few men in this fort who will question whether you might be actually involved in the ambush itself."

"How about ye, Colonel?" Perez's soft interruption was backed by a look as sharp as a split rock.

Clanton took the look and the question, slowly. "Pawnee, I know you're a brave man. There's no question of cowardice here. As to the ambush, I don't know. But for the time being, and from my viewpoint, these things are the least of it."

"Whut's the most of it, Colonel?" The half-breed's words dropped into the following pause with snowflake stillness.

"The most of it, Perez, is that as an enlisted soldier in the United States Army you are fully aware of military regulations." The Post Commander pushed back from his desk, came shoulder-braced and scowling to his feet. "*No soldier may run out in the face of action. Nor refuse to follow the orders of any superior officer in the field—no matter how rash or ill-considered those orders may appear to him to be at the time.*

"I don't have to tell you what the Army calls such conduct. Nor what the sentence for that conduct is. Nor that, in this case and in my opinion, you would fully deserve that sentence. I'm sorry, Perez. The charge is *desertion!*"

"Is thet all, Colonel?"

"Not quite." The scout's low-voiced query brought Clanton leaning over the desk, smooth jaw trap-set. "If Stacey gets out, all right; and in view of your previous service, we'll leave it at simple desertion. That's five years. If he doesn't, Perez," the colonel's blue eyes went flat-cold, "*I'm going to hang you.*"

"Whut about meantime, Colonel?"

"Meantime, you're under post arrest. You will have the freedom of the fort until further developments. That's all."

96

"I allow ye'd best not worry about me, Colonel. This fort'll be under hostile siege by nightfall. When chiefs the size of Red Cloud, Dull Knife, Little Wolf and Man-Afraid get together under Crazy Hoss, it ain't no raid. Hawk Creighton's two thousand warriors was accurate. Happen ye'd best believe thet."

"Frankly, I've lost faith in you, man. When Creighton gets back, we'll see. But God help you if anything happens to Stacey."

"Don't worry about Stacey, nor Creighton neither. They're done fer." The half-breed scout spoke on, unfeelingly, his narrowed eyes as far away as his ranging, red thoughts. "Likely, ye'd best jest buy my story the way I give it to ye. Then start yer dispatch riders fer the Muleshoe Crick telegraph station while they kin still git out'n the fort. Come dark ye're goin' to have Sioux ringed around hyar so tight ye cain't spit without ye git some of it on them. And come daylight the snow'll be wind-piled over the tops of yer north and east gates. Ye won't be able to open them wide enough to pitch a cat out'n, let alone pass a hoss and rider."

"Nonsense, Perez." Colonel Clanton's denial moved on uneasy feet. "We'll be perfectly all right as soon as Tendrake brings Stacey in."

"If he brings him in, it'll be acrost a hoss's withers, with his haid skun closer'n a peeled polecat's."

"Dammit, Perez!"—irritation replaced the uncertainty—"they'll be all right. Tendrake will get them back in."

"Supposin' he don't?"

"I don't suppose things, man," the colonel's conclusion brittled up. "Now, get yourself something to eat—and stay around barracks until I send for you. You'll find Mrs. Collins and the women serving hot food in the kitchen. Get along."

Shaking his lean head hopelessly, Perez slunk across the calf-deep snows of the parade yard. Beyond, he could just make out the sick yellow windows of the company kitchens. The cold, intense all day, was deepening now. It bit into a man that hard it left tooth marks. Zero, anyway, thought Perez, and dropping by the minute. Ahead, the rough log door of the kitchens jumped at him, through the white smother.

Inside, he found Lura Collins and accepted the mug of bitter, black Arbuckle's she brought him, with one of his rare flash-smiles. While he drank, she sat on the bench across

97

the table from him, her almond-green eyes regarding him steadily. "How about some hot slum, Pawnee?" she asked, shortly.

"I cain't eat," said Perez, his black glance returning her stare. "My belly's knotted up like a colicky calf's gut."

"What's eating you, Pawnee? You look sort of funny, sort of frightened, maybe. I've never seen you scared. You *are* afraid, aren't you, Pawnee?" Her voice, instantly low, went out to the swart half-breed like a soft, white hand.

"Yeah, I'm afraid, ma'am."

"Why? Don't tell me the great Pawnee Perez is afraid of Indians?" Her laugh went with the rest of her; gay, bubbly, warm; yet woman-sounding enough to raise the hackles on any man that was half a he-dog. And, too, her eyes needled him with the words. There was something hard about this girl that fascinated Perez.

Lura Collins wasn't like the other women of the fort. To them, Pawnee Perez was an evil half-breed, the sort of man one hurried the children past, and heard their husbands call "that damn, black breed of the colonel's." But to Lura, Perez felt he was something beyond his mixed blood and dark appearance. Not a pretty man, Pawnee Perez, not a nice man, perhaps even, by white standards, a very bad man. But to Lura Collins, and her kind the world over, such as Perez would always be at least one thing, and just one thing—a *man*.

Lura's life at the fort these six months following the death of Lieutenant Collins had been a strange one. No one knew why she stayed or why the colonel allowed her to stay. The women had all felt she had her "nasty green eyes on the major's oak leaves, and with poor Lieutenant Collins not six months in his tragic gravel" Consequently, colonel's daughter or no, they had given her a very cold time of it.

But the red-haired girl had set about making herself a place on the post. She petted the other women through their cramps, sat their children, did their fancy sewing and frontier dressmaking all to such good effect that she shortly had the officers' wives as firmly wrapped around her slender finger as she did their husbands' eyes around her equally slender figure.

Within thirty days of her arrival, she had progressed from the vinegar-tongued classification of "that redheaded slut" to the syrupy safety of "that poor, dear Mrs. Collins!"

Watching her now, Perez knew all the excitement of that months-gone day when he had headed her drunken "hus-

98

band's" troops in the fight that saved her life; remembered, clean to the toes of his buffalo-hock boots, the lifting rush of blood that had come as he'd stepped across Lieutenant Collins' form to take her in his arms. Remembered, too, the driving pressure of those molded hips coming into him with the kiss. And the swelling form of the big breasts crushing hard and full against the broad leanness of his chest. And the pure, crazy fire of the kiss itself, making him grind his wide mouth into her full, soft one, grind into it until his teeth smashed into hers and the maddening, salt taste of the blood from her bitten lip was running in his mouth.

Since that time, apparently by deliberate and cool contrivance of the girl, the half-breed and Lura had seen little of each other. From her obvious actions Perez could have thought that they had never met, let alone stood in straining embrace. But when they did meet, their glances never failed to lock, and being the kind of man he was, Perez knew he was looking at a woman—his kind of woman. Not once had her eyes failed to receipt his hard stares with melting interest.

"Ma'am," the bearded scout spoke at last, "I'll tell ye somethin'. Thet Major Stacey and all the men with him is dead."

At the girl's involuntary gasp, his thin face twisted. "Shet up. I want ye to listen, and to keep yer ears uncovered while ye are, and to recollect thet it's me, Pawnee Perez, whut's doin' the talkin'."

She nodded, her slanting eyes wide, full mouth parted. The half-breed went on, hurrying his words, now. "If Captain Tendrake gits back and brings in this report on Stacey gittin' wiped out, which he will, ma'am, Colonel Clanton's goin' to guardhouse me. I'm sayin' fer ye to remember me if thet happens."

"What do you mean?" The girl glanced nervously at the other women in the room. "Hurry, Pawnee, they're watching us. How can I do anything for you if my father does put you under guard? I can't influence him and—"

"I ain't talkin' particular about him. I mean the others. Ye kin do anything ye want"—the breed paused, meaningfully, black eyes glittering as they trapped hers—"with any man on this post!"

"Except my father." Lura Collins was returning his stare, full measure.

"Except nobody," snapped Perez. "Jest remember whut I said. This place is goin' to be in the middle of hell with the

99

lights turned out—and damn soon. When it gits dark, ye remember Perez!"

The girl flushed. "I've got to go. The mother hens are beginning to cluck. I'll get you some more coffee."

"The hell with the coffee. I'm goin' over and camp on yer old man's doorstep. It's four, now. If Tendrake's comin' back at all, it should ought to be soon. I want to be thar when he makes his talk." Coming up off the bench and around the corner of the crude plank table in one sinuous move, the breed grabbed the startled girl by the arm. His long fingers clamped into the soft flesh with numbing fierceness.

"Remember me," he said, and was gone, even before she knew he had hurt her arm.

Perez had no more than left the kitchens when a commotion sprang up along the north stockade. The scout could see nothing, but a lull in the wind brought the deadened reports of three or four shots fired from the top of the wall. These were answered from outside the fort by a male bovine bellow which could have originated only in the hairy chest of a bull buffalo or the rawhide-lined lungs of a certain Hibernian company sergeant. A haunting trace of Celtic delicacy in the inhuman roar ruled out the buffalo.

"Hold yer fire, yez cross-eyed apes! Since when has Crazy Harse bin wearin' a sargint's stripes and sportin' hisself a head of lovely red hair?"

A minute later Perez was helping force the gates ajar for Sergeant Murdo Murphy and his survivors to stagger through.

The scout had guessed right about Murphy's attackers leaving him and the Bay Horse Meadow fight, to join the main ambush on Stacey. The sergeant had abandoned his wagons, making it into the fort on foot, under cover of the storm. A high plains blizzard can be a warm friend as well as a bitter-cold enemy, as ten lucky privates and one red-thatched sergeant would testify for the rest of their lives.

The gates had scarcely closed on the hay train survivors when they opened to admit Captain Tendrake and his fifty infantry, frozen not alone from their twelve-mile march up and back the Virginia City Road. Their frost-rimmed eyes had beheld sight enough to chill every man in the company long past the memory of any storm. Five minutes after their return, an exhausted, horrified Captain Tendrake was gulping brandy and gritting out the details of his bloody find. Perez was present, as were Sergeants Simpson and Murphy, and Captain Howell.

100

Tendrake went through his story, almost without taking a breath, his low voice and halting diction reflecting the paralysis of the shock he was under. "When I reached Eagle Point the snow was beginning in earnest. I could still see down Squaw Pine Ridge to Peyo Creek Flats. At least two thousand Indians were galloping their horses around on the flats.

"When they saw us, they set up a howl. We found out soon enough what they were howling about. Two hundred feet down the ridge, we found the cavalry. A group of ten bodies, first, then, lower down, a group of twenty. There were empty cartridge cases heaped around in drifts. And there was blood, pools of it. A lot of it, apparently, Indian blood.

"All the bodies were scalped and mutilated.

"As we waited there, not knowing what to do, the hostiles started up the ridge toward us. Two main chiefs led the advance. One was a very big man, wearing a scarlet blanket, riding a spotted stallion. The other was a small man, very straight on his horse, dressed in black furs. He was riding Major Stacey's sockfoot bay—"

"Red Cloud and Crazy Horse," interjected Perez, letting the names come through teeth.

Tendrake seemed not to have heard the half-breed, continuing his narrative in the flat monotone of shock. "I retreated at once. As soon as they saw me get to the ridgetop, they split and went down both sides of the ridge, disappearing in the timber. I expected an ambush on the way back but nothing happened. We didn't see an Indian.

"On the way up I met Perez, here, who told me he had deserted Stacey before the fight began. He warned me back and told me Stacey would be dead before I reached him.

"God help you now, Perez," the captain concluded, turning, gray-faced, on the scout. "Eighty white men shot and hacked to pieces out there. And you left them when you knew what they were going into, when you might still have helped them. The white man doesn't live who could look you in the face after that. May God have mercy on your miserable soul. No man in this fort ever will."

"Amen!" sneered Perez, disgustedly, the muscles of his jaw clamping set. "Trouble with ye Army boys is ye've all read too many Wild Bill Hickok stories. Ye quit lookin' at them goddam Ned Buntline books and ye'll do better. Happen the way things come out, yer Major Stacey was a hoss's ass. He was a goddam fool and he kilt all them good men under him."

Colonel Clanton and Captain Tendrake showed signs of

rising to the defense of the hero dead and the honor of the Army, but Sergeant Murphy, his Irish soul sensitive to the horror of the carnage on the ridge, breathed a quiet thought which brought the minds of all to bear on the realities of the moment. "Glory to God," muttered the old soldier, "the whole splendid lot of them byes dead and scalped in the snow. . . ."

Realization comes to a dull man slowly, but it comes hard at last. Clanton's question was laced with despair. "Tendrake. Howell. What in God's name are we going to do?"

Captain James Howell, cool and bright-hard as Perez had figured him, took over.

"Put every man on the stockades. Free the prisoners. Arm every man. Packers, clerks, blacksmiths, carpenters, storekeepers. The whole damn bunch. Wire the powder magazine and put the women and children inside. If the hostiles get over the stockade—blow the magazine."

"How about this man?" Tendrake's query indicated Perez.

"I said, every man," snapped Howell. "We can worry about his goddam morals if we live to do it. And for my pay"—the atmosphere, growing more brittle by the minute, was strained to the last nerve—"the breed is more than half right about Stacey. You can stuff that in your pipes, all of you!"

"All right, Howell." Colonel Clanton was getting into his coat, ignoring the flat challenge of the captain's hard-boiled backing of Perez. "Let's go. But the half-breed is under arrest and that's final. Clear out the guardhouse if you will, but Perez stays in it and that's an order!"

"Don't be a fool!" There are fighting men to whom rank means nothing when the lead has started to fly. Howell was one of them. "This man is the best shot in the stockade, the best Indian fighter on the Powder River."

"I don't give a damn if he's the second coming of Davy Crockett, I won't have him loose in this fort!" Clanton, his phlegmaticism for once bristled with excitement, was shouting. "Lock him up and leave him locked up!"

Perez spoke once, then kept silent. "I'd like to fight fer ye, Colonel. Ye kin have my word about escapin'. And no man, breed or white, should ought to be locked up with there bein' a chancet of Crazy Hoss gittin' over the stockade."

"Damn right! That's pretty raw, even for a half-breed." Howell's sharp agreement sided with the copper-skinned scout.

"Half-breed, whole-breed, what's the difference? This is a

treacherous man and I won't trust him again. Lock him up, Howell. Right now!"

I'll take him over," Tendrake offered. "Let Howell look to the stockade. I'll get the other prisoners out and put Perez away."

"Good." Clanton's voice crawled higher with tension. "Come on, Howell. Let's go." Hurrying out the door, however, his eagles banged once more against the captain's bars.

"You get the women and children into the magazine, Colonel," Howell directed, quietly, "I'll see to the walls by myself."

Tendrake, once Clanton and Howell were gone, spoke wearily to Murphy. "Come on, Sergeant, let's take the prisoner over."

"Yes, sir," answered the latter, watching the half-breed as he spoke.

Perez had no intention of going into that cell block. The scout had a normal aversion to dying in any form, but to be cooped up, weaponless, in a six-by-eight cell in a fortress that was apt to be deep in hostiles before the sun got up, was precisely his last idea of the way to make the big jump. Even as Captain Tendrake spoke to Murphy, the half-breed's quick glance darted around the room. Where a neat hand could set a trap, a wary foot could still avoid it. A man could only try, leastways. The door was still open—

But other heads, older in the business than Tendrake's, were in the colonel's office. As Perez' muscles tensed for the lunge at the weary captain, standing, unarmed, in the beckoning doorway, the scout felt the Colt jam into his back.

"Let's not try it now, Perez lad. Go along, gentle-like, eh? Shure, I feel sorry fer yez, but orders is orders."

The half-breed had some working knowledge of Sergeant Murdo Murphy's abilities in a fight: at the same time the tail of his roving eye caught Sergeant Simpson sliding around Colonel Clanton's desk, picking a Spencer out of the wall rack.

"Let's go," he shrugged, resignedly.

"Shure now, and thet's the way to talk," clucked Murphy. "Ye'll just walk along, easy-like, and none of yer Injun tricks, eh, lad?" The sergeant gave the Colt in the scout's back just the nuance of a two-hundred-pound shove. "One little move and ye'll find me finger to be as light on this trigger as the kiss of a feather on a virgin's veranda."

"Ye talk a lot, Murphy," grunted Perez, and started moving

for the door. Outside, the scout thought, in the choke of that wind and snow, much could happen. It was a hundred yards across the parade yard. Many a man's fortune had twisted in ten.

But Perez was wrong. Sergeant Murdo Murphy had as heavy a hand as he did a light trigger finger. Withal, he kept shoving the Colt so hard into the scout's kidneys as to keep Perez glancing down at his bellybutton, momentarily expecting to see the muzzle of the weapon protruding from his lean navel.

Inside the prison building, Murphy prodded the half-breed into the nearest empty cell, refusing even to turn him over to the corporal of the guard. "Yez jest help the captain to release the other prisoners, dearie," he cooed to that individual. "I'll incarcyrate this little man, meself."

Within the cell, Perez sighed with relief. "Lookit ye, now, Murphy. One more jab in the bladder with thet hand-size field gun of yers, and ye'll have me wettin' my leggins from belt to brisket. Ease off a mite, eh, friend?"

"Shure, lad," the sergeant's accents were apologetic. " 'Twas none of my doin's. I don't believe ye're the dirty slob yez profess to me, but I'm only a sargint."

"Yeah, sure, Murphy. We're friends. Now, ye jest remember Perez when the hostiles get over the stockade. If ye're too busy to git in hyar with a key, jest say a couple of Hail Marys fer me."

"Faith, now, Mister Perez, yez don't really think the reds scuts will git over, do yez?"

"They kin if they want to. In twenty-four hours thet snow'll be driv so high agin them north and east walls, they kin walk up the drifts and step over the top logs."

"The saints pertect us, I—" Murphy's supplication was rudely interrupted.

"Come on, Sergeant!" Captain Tendrake's irritation was compounded by fatigue. "Let's get these other men out of here. The Old Man wants them all armed and on the stockade in ten minutes. You and your Sioux friend can continue your admiration society meeting later."

Perez watched, emotionless, as the two sergeants, Murphy and Simpson, herded the prisoners out into the snow. Tendrake took even the guard corporal along, leaving the scout with nothing but a plethora of iron bars and a paucity of sputtering stove-fire for company.

104

One look around Clanton's guardhouse was enough to let the prisoner know that Lura Collins was his one key. If nothing else, Perez mused, Clanton was a piss-cutter of an engineer. It would take a drunk grizzly with a hard hangover and six crowbars the best part of a long winter to crack out of that cell block. The half-breed was something of a connoisseur of frontier detention structures, having studied some of the more classic examples from the inside out. A greased rat couldn't have gotten out of this one without he had somebody to give him a stiff shove in the butt.

To the frozen watchers on the stockade, it seemed God had forgotten Fort Will Farney. Numbed alike by the ferocious cold and the crawling memory of Stacey's massacre, the men manned the catwalks and lower rifle slits like dumb cattle awaiting the approach of the slaughterer.

The cold, itself, was an enemy to match any red foe for fierceness. The instant a man stepped into it, his nostrils were driven flat together and sealed shut as though by the grip of a giant's fingers. To breathe, a man had to open his mouth, literally gasping to get the air in, then, deprived of any warming progress through the nose passages, the inhalation struck his lungs, frost-cold. Fifty breaths and a man's chest ached that bad he could scarce draw the fifty-first. Within ten minutes of leaving shelter, his hands were feelingless to the wrists, his feet numbed stumps upon which his best progress could be a lurching, blind stumble. In twenty, the frost had gone to his shoulders and knees, leaving him to clump along the icy catwalks like an armless stilt-walker.

No soldier could stand more than thirty minutes of such exposure and be left active. In such temperatures a man could barely hold on to a rifle, let alone operate one. And there was a tragic joker in this cold deck—Clanton's fuel supply was dangerously low. The Sioux had caught him with barely half his winter's wood hauled in from the cutting sites. He had plenty to keep the kitchens and main barracks going for a week. After that, provided they hadn't found a quicker way meantime, the hostiles had but to wait for their ice-bellied ally, Wasiya, to reduce the garrison for them.

And if the wood were the joker in Clanton's misdealt deck, the water was the wild card. What they could melt from the snow inside the fort, they had; always remembering that it used up precious fuel to melt it. When wood and snow were gone, Sam-ya Ceze-t'e, Blackened Tongues, the Thirst Devil, would come to squat at Wasiya's side. And at whose side Wasiya squatted was at Red Cloud's and at Crazy Horse's sides.

This and other pleasant prospects gamboled happily through the colonel's mind as he and his officers huddled in the watch hut at the north gate, while behind the confused tangle of these front-running thoughts another thought stalked, darkly: Perez, the suspected traitor, the dark-skinned Pawnee half-breed, had foretold every item on the ledger of fear now fronting the Commanding Officer of Fort Will Farney. Clanton remembered, now, and clearly, the urgency with which the scout had counseled him to get his wood and hay into the stockade ahead of all other tasks, and above all, to build a fort wing enclosing a strip of Spruce Creek.

But where this back-of-the-mind knowledge might have caused a more emotional man to reconsider his judgment of the scout, its presence in Colonel Clanton's thoughts only added to his general confusion, causing the plodding officer deliberately to bury it under a mental manure pile of his own belief in his personal rightness, this to clear his limited capacity for thinking in terms of such immediate lines of military action as might be taken to resolve the garrison's present extreme danger.

"What time is it now?" Clanton directed the question aimlessly.

"Two A.M.," answered Captain Howell.

"Eight hours since Tendrake got back, and no sign of the Sioux yet!" The Colonel did his best to find a little heart in the fact. The others failed to take fire.

"And none of your missing scout, Hawk Creighton, either." This, from Howell, dry-voiced. "I guess the half-breed was right about him, anyway."

"He was right about poor Stacey, too." Tendrake's interjection was bitter.

Howell ignored the obvious interpretation of Tendrake's lament, continuing bluntly, "He's been right about most things he's spoken up on, since I've been on the post."

"Yes, he has," agreed Clanton, seriously. "But you can't trust a man like that. Twice now he's put himself under suspicion of guiding white men into Indian traps. With his half-blood background, we can't look at him as we might a fellow white. I don't mean I discriminate against him on that score, but he has told me of his birth among the Pawnees and his upbringing among the Sioux and Cheyenne. That red

106

color rubs off, and much as I like Perez as a man, it appears to me that quite a lot of that color has rubbed off on him."

"Appearances have hanged many an innocent man." Howell was carelessly passing rank again. "The breed's half Indian and doesn't see things our way. That doesn't make him wrong. Personally, I think he sees them a lot better. I'm new on this post but not to this country nor its people. I've been up here before. I'll say I know Indians better than any man in this fort except Perez. And I say he's clearly not working with the hostiles. The Indian mind, in the tactical sense, doesn't go that deep, Colonel. They don't infiltrate and sabotage an enemy before they hit him, the way we whites try to do. I think this half-breed is trying to be a white man, and doing a whole hell of a lot better job of it than some of us. And I think he ought to be out here, with us, with a gun in his hand and a tongue in this council. Now, what do you think of that?"

"Hang it all, Jim, if I let him out he'd be just as apt to go over the stockade and join the hostiles as not. And we can't chance that. I agree with you that he's a first-class fighting man and a smart, dangerous thinker. That's just exactly why I'm not going to turn him loose. He knows this fort as well as I do, remember that. He watched every log of it go in place. If he got out to the hostiles there's no telling how he might use that knowledge."

"Oh hell!"—this vehemently from Howell. "You've let Stacey poison you on the man. I trust I don't belittle the major's heroic memory when I remind you that he conducted himself like an utter fool today. It's clear he bolted his orders exactly as Perez charges, and that he, and he alone, bears full responsibility for the loss of his command. No thinking man could seriously suspect Perez had anything to do with that ambush. He certainly didn't ask to guide the party. Damn it all, that breed was just too Indian-smart to go down that ridge with Stacey. If it's a crime not to be a damn fool, then Perez is guilty. Otherwise you've got nothing on him that you can make stick five minutes in a military inquiry. Personally, I don't think you can even hang desertion on him."

Colonel Clanton was too confused to rise to this challenge of his opinion and actions. He barged ahead with his own lead-footed line of thought, ambiguously continuing to include the half-breed in it. "Perez thought we should get dispatch riders off for the Muleshoe Creek telegraph station before the Sioux could get into position around the fort. But damn it, we haven't even seen an Indian since this morning. I can't be calling up relief from Fort Loring for a siege that hasn't even started yet. They'd laugh me out of the service." Stomping bluntly along this track, the fort commander began to listen to his own arguments. "Why, I'll wager the Sioux have already retired, gone north or wherever the devil it was Creighton said their camp was."

"I'll go with you on that, Colonel." Tendrake's support was more hopeful than reasonable. "This whole thing will blow over with the storm." Uneasiness added a hedger to the captain's optimism. "But perhaps it would be a good idea to send a rider down to Muleshoe to at least alert Fort Loring."

"Sorry, gentlemen"—Captain James Howell was a taciturn man, a very competent officer, one who'd been on the frontier longer than Tendrake and Colonel Clanton combined—"your lively conclusions are dead wrong. It's already too late to get a rider out."

"What the devil do you mean, Howell?" The C.O.'s question sprouted the wings of real alarm. "You haven't given up, have you, man?"

"Not quite, Colonel Clanton," replied the younger officer, grimly. "But half an hour ago, when I came on watch, God hauled off and gave me a look at something."

"Such as?" Tendrake crowded him tersely.

"One of those freak clear spots broke a hole in the storm. For a minute or two I could see black sky and stars, maybe for about one-third of the compass, southeast, south, southwest."

"Well, what of it?" Clanton's patience was going, his query rising on a voice-crack of irritation.

"Well, black sky and stars wasn't all I saw. Smoke, too, gentlemen. Lots of it. As far as I saw. Thin spirals and wisps of it. Blue-gray. Wood smoke. The kind that crawls up out of Sioux lodge smoke-holes on just such a deep winter evening. We're surrounded."

"Oh, my God," exploded Tendrake, "that finishes us!"

"No! No, it doesn't! There's still a chance for outside help." Clanton's surprise statement jumped with sudden hope.

"How so?" Howell queried.

"I just remembered Bailey and O'Connor. They're sure to stop at Muleshoe Station and telegraph Colonel Boynton at Fort Loring. Surely they'd think of that, don't you think, Howell?" Relief spurred the commander's conclusions. "Why,

108

it's entirely possible that Boynton may have already started a column up."

"It won't wash, Colonel." Howell was curt. "I agree that Bailey and O'Connor would logically make for Muleshoe Creek as the nearest Army post. And I agree that if they got there, the noncom in charge would telegraph Fort Loring. But let's take a hard look.

"All the hostiles Bailey and O'Connor saw were Black Shield's three hundred Minniconjou. That's all they could report. You've got a garrison that size, here. Those scouts didn't know a damn thing about Stacey's massacre.

"Now, suppose Boynton did get their report by telegraph from Muleshoe. And even suppose he was mildly alarmed by it. Don't you think he'd still be awaiting a confirmation from you on it? Let's remember the dear old Army, sir. Three copies of everything and a brigadier's personal signature before a corporal can go to the latrine by himself.

"And let's always remember that Bailey and O'Connor may never have gotten to Muleshoe. The Sioux understand telegraph, too, Colonel."

"They're our only chance, anyway," Clanton's mutter was peevish, "and I choose to think they made it and that Boynton got our message. Why, even without a confirmation, he'll begin to wonder at our silence sooner or later. Why, in a few days, two weeks at the most, he'll—"

"And just where the hell do you think we'll be in two weeks, Colonel?"

Clanton didn't come back at Howell's interruptive challenge, contenting himself with repeating his hope for Bailey and O'Connor. "I don't care. I still think those two scouts are our only chance."

"Our only chance," Howell contradicted him, "is still the one Perez gave you—to get a rider out to Muleshoe Creek. We can hang on here for a week, likely. Maybe two, three days longer. If a rider could get through, it would give us a chance. We might just stick it till Boynton got up here, or at least close enough to let the Sioux know he was coming. It's a hell of a chance, I'll admit."

"I won't order any man on such a ride, Howell. Even if I did, how would you propose making him go? Any man in his right mind would rather be shot, outright, than fall into the hands of the hostiles. And beyond the Indians, what about that blizzard out there? It's one hundred and ninety miles to Muleshoe Creek Station. In this weather any order to try and ride there would amount to a death sentence. Have you looked at a thermometer in the last hour, Captain?"

"Thirty below, when I came in. But, damn it to hell, if it was ninety below, somebody's got to make that ride. If you won't order a man we'll have to ask for volunteers. There's a lot of men in this stockade, Colonel, with their wives and children sitting in that wired powder magazine. You'll get your volunteer."

Clanton was silent a moment before answering. "All right. Call a muster of the sergeants for ten minutes—in the kitchens. I'll see you there."

With the older man gone, Captain Tendrake turned to his companion. "You won't get your volunteer, Jim. Every man in this fort is scared blue, clear down to his toenails. That goes for me, too. If a man could see a possible chance of getting through—why, sure. But with that snow out there you can't see a foot. You wouldn't know where you were, except you'd know that sooner or later you were going to step on two thousand Indians. Women and children, hell. Who wants to kill himself just to show he wasn't afraid to try?"

"Come on," Howell's order was abrupt. "Let's get those sergeants in to the Old Man. You take the east wall, I'll get the west."

"Right," sighed Tendrake, wearily. "See you inside."

Colonel Clanton and his two captains waited in the kitchens. There was no talk, now, each of them sitting, impassive, thinking his own thoughts, listening with his own ears to the hungry yammer of the great storm outside.

The sergeants had been briefed on asking for volunteers and sent on out to query their individual outfits, Murphy having been detailed to collect their findings and report back to the kitchens. The minutes stretched from ten to fifteen to twenty, and still no Murphy. At half an hour he stomped in, hoarfrost and caked snow encrusting every inch of his figure.

"Faith and bejabbers if thet thermometer on the north gate ain't standin' at forty below! Holy Mither, whut a foin night fer a massacree."

"Faith, and ye weren't sent out to check the timperature," mimicked Captain Howell acidly, his demanding stare boring at the old sergeant.

Murphy stood irresolute, head bowed, fur cap in hand.

110

"Shure now, Captain, yez can't blame the lads." It passed unnoticed that the noncom ignored Clanton. "It's a howlin', arful storm out there, and—"

"No takers, is that it, Sergeant?" Howell cut him short.

"Thet's it, sir. There ain't a enlisted man in the fort to do yer ridin' fer yez. We checked them all, twoice."

"Well," the captain's laugh was short, "that leaves us, the noble officers."

"It leaves you," said Tendrake, unhesitatingly. "I wouldn't leave this fort for all the wives and children in Wyoming."

"And I can't," echoed Clanton, dully.

"I can"—Howell's reaction carried no heroics—"and I will. How about it, Colonel?"

Clanton looked at him, wagging his big head. "No, you know better than that, Jim. I don't even appreciate the offer. You know I can't spare you. You're the only one here that really knows these hostiles. Let's be reasonable."

"Then there's no one to go and we can just sit here and wait for Crazy Horse to come and get us."

"I can't see anything else at the moment, Jim." Clanton's voice wasn't two tones off the minor discord of despair. "We sit and wait. And when they come at us, we fight. Meantime we pray for Bailey and O'Connor. There's no one to make the ride, now, and—"

When the interruption came, it was the surprise cloak of the low voice of Lura Collins.

The colonel's daughter had refused to share the shelter of the powder magazine and, demonstrating Perez' claim that she could do anything with any man on the post, not excepting her father, she had prevailed on the commander with the argument that her presence in the kitchens would serve better than coffee to keep the men warm. Clanton was not blind to the power the girl held for men, nor to the reason and sense behind her claim. He'd given in almost without firing a shot. Now, unnoticed, Lura had come up to stand behind the officers.

"You're forgetting someone, Dad—"

Colonel Clanton looked up, annoyed. "Oh, hello, Lura. No coffee, thank you, dear. We are too—"

"What did you say, ma'am?" Captain Howell overrode his superior, shooting his question directly to the girl. His quick mind had caught her statement, was already running stirrup to stirrup with her thoughts.

111

"I said, you're forgetting the best man on the post, Captain." The eyes were seriously wide, the petulant mouth parted with excitement.

"You mean Perez, naturally."

"Naturally. He's just a half-breed, of course," Lura let the words fall with scalding slowness, "but he's a *man*. He'll make your ride for you. Unless, of course, the competition is limited to pure-breds."

No one answered the girl, the silence following her outburst serving only to highlight the subdued mutterings of the fire at the far end of the room and the rising howl of the blizzard outside.

That blizzard of '66 carried many a two-legged destiny in its frozen belly—and one four-legged one.

In his deep-strawed box stall, Kentucky Boy stirred restlessly. The big stallion was used to the kind of king's treatment which went with being the C.O.'s personal pleasure mount, and now he wasn't getting it!

Kentucky Boy was a bluegrass thoroughbred, a tall, flashy, blood-bay, sixteen hands at the withers, deep through the heart, big-barreled, long-ribbed, short-backed. A hot-blooded horse, Kentucky Boy, thirteen hundred pounds of line-bred bone, muscle, satin skin, clean limbs, powerful body; a violent-tempered brute, nervous, taut, willful; withal, a man's horse, iron-jawed, velvet-mouthed, with lungs as big as a buffalo's and a heart as brave as a bear's; a fierce, vain, six-year-old studhorse, with a fifteen-foot stride and the bred-in bottom to hold on it till his heart broke or his arteries burst.

The big bay stallion had not been ridden in three days, nor fed in the past twenty-four hours. He missed his groom, his rolled oats, bran, currycomb, workouts. His normal bad temper was inflamed to the point of fury. He slammed the thin bar plates of his rear heels repeatedly into the sides of the stall, lashed out at the stable door with angry forefeet, bit savagely at the wood of his manger, kicked his water bucket three times around the stall, stomped its oaken staves flat with jabbing forefoot blows. After that, he just stood there, spraddle-legged, ears back, eyes rolling, blasting the quiet of the stable building with a series of whistling stallion neighs.

He whistled in vain. Outside, the storm whistled louder. His challenge went unheard. Outside, every human ear was bent to receive another, fiercer challenge—the eerie war-cry of the High Plains Sioux.

Kentucky Boy stopped neighing and listened: a half-dozen answering whinnies down the line of coarse-headed cavalry geldings, and then nothing. The bay stallion blew out, loudly, fell to pacing his stall, whickering and grunting nervously.

Beyond his split-log stable, a two-legged animal was putting her white shoulder to the course of destiny, turning its path aside, twisting it straight around for the stall door of Fort Will Farney's final, four-legged chance.

Lura Collins came into the guardhouse, quickly, the sucking force of the following wind slamming the door behind her with bar-rattling force.

"*Hohahe!* Welcome to my tipi!" said Perez, in Sioux, grinning. "What time is it?"

"About three. I brought you some coffee."

"Meat, too, I see. Put it on the table, and get me out of hyar. Keys are in the guard desk, top draw. Hurry up."

"I didn't come to get you out, Pawnee. I only—"

"Git them keys, girl!" The half-breed's eyes were slitted. "Ye're not goin' to let Perez die in hyar."

"No, I know that." The admission was helpless, the long-lashed eyes lingering on the scout. "So do you, Pawnee."

"Yeah, I allow I do. Git them keys."

Shrugging off her heavy wrap, the girl searched the desk. "They aren't here, Perez!"

"Grab thet Spencer out'n the guard rack. Pass it in hyar."

The three shots reverberated dully in the empty building. Perez stepped through the gun smoke, grabbed the food, began wolfing it. Sailing the lid of the coffee tin across the room, he gulped directly from the steaming container. "Now, listen," he grunted between smacking mouthfuls, "and listen good."

The girl nodded, breathless.

"Ye git out'n hyar, right now. Git me gloves and grub, fur gloves and about four pounds of jerky. Some hardtack, too. I want one of yer father's coats, thar's two, three of them hangin' in his office. I want a garrison hat like he wears. Thet's the winter-blue, with the ear flaps. The colonel he don't drink but ye've got to git me whiskey. Try Howell's quarters. He 'pears man enough to handle a bottle. Put the whiskey in a canteen, all ye kin git of it. One thing other. I want a bucket of hot water. Ye got all thet?"

"Gloves, coat, hat, hot water, jerky—" gasped the girl.

113

"And whiskey!" snapped Perez. "Fer Christ's sake, don't fergit the whiskey."

Barking his words, the scout gave her the layout of the stables. "Thar's two rows of single stalls, tackroom, vet's stall, stable sergeant's quarters. Next to them's a big box stall fer the colonel's hoss, thet big ornery bay bastard. Ye got thet, now?"

"You mean Kentucky Boy!" The girl's eyes were dark with excitement.

"Thet's the hoss. Kin ye git down thar with all the gear in ten minutes?"

"Why, Pawnee, why? What are you going to do?"

"I'm gittin' out'n hyar, thet's all. Ye're he'pin' me on account ye owe me one. Thet's how it is, ain't it?"

She looked at him a long second, the lovely face going suddenly hard as she dropped her eyes.

"Yes, that's the way it is. And I'll do it." She looked back up at him, all the warmth her eyes had held for him gone out like snow-snuffed coals. "I'll get the things for you, Perez."

"Ye'd best," the scout flashed her a grimace, more grim than grin, "or the next hand on thet white butt of yers is apt to be a red one!"

Lura, missing the real implication in his words, blanched. "Why, you dirty, foul-mouthed half—"

"Don't ye say it!" rapped Perez. "Ye call me a half-breed and I'll smash yer pale face up agin thet wall. Goddam ye, I'll do it!" The scout's thin jaw was writhing, his strange eyes glittering, his voice going back to its purring softness, even as he spoke. "I cain't take thet off'n ye, girl." He had her then, long hands clamping her arms close up to the shoulders, cruel thumbs and fingers meeting and locking in the warm prisons of her armpits.

"Pawnee! Don't!" The cry was one of real fear. "You're hurting me. Oh, Pawnee, you're hurting me. Please!"

He stood back, the breath whistling in his nostrils, head bowed, face dark-flushed. A second fled, then another. He didn't look up until he heard the first sob.

When he did look, he saw the bare whiteness of her arm where his grasp had shredded the rough linsey blouse, the blue of the finger marks already darkening. He saw, too, the mouth-parted expression of fear, the shadow of pain darkening the green eyes, the bright glitter of the tear as it hesitated under the curling lash.

"Ma'am, God he'p me, ma'am. I love ye."

114

"Perez—!"

"I know, girl. Ye don't need to tell me. But I'm glad ye never said it. Ye jest fergit whut I said. A man gets crazy around a woman like ye, thet's all. I've had ye inside of me ever since I first smelled ye in thet damn tent back thar in Red Cloud's meadow. When I teched ye thar in the dark, the fire run up my arm like I'd seized on to a burnin' chunk. I dropped ye quick, girl, but the searin' ain't never healed. It ain't never stopped hurtin'. I allow I'm no good the way ye count men, not even if I was pure white. Ye'd never have no life with me but a squaw's. I don't know no other and I ain't built fer no other. I got to be out whar the wind kin blow thet hard it'll knock a strong pony's laigs right out'n from under him, or so soft it kin kiss ye lighter'n young lips their first night. I got to be whar I kin hit the stars by swingin' a short lance. Whar ye kin smell the September hay mixed thet sweet with the buffalo droppin's and the pony-herd dung, as to lump up a prairie man's th'oat so's he cain't hardly swaller. Whar ye kin git a hoss atwixt yer laigs, or a woman, either, any time ye wants them, and still not be pullin' no travois when the short grass fuzzes up green in the spring."

The half-breed had been looking down all the while, running his words fast and low. Now he looked up, saw the dumb misery in the girl's face, read the dry hardness in her eyes, dropped his gaze and his voice once more.

"I bin tellin' ye I love ye, girl. I had to let it out'n me. I never told no other woman thet, fer I never felt it fer no other one."

"Perez—" she interrupted him. "It's no use, *Shacun.*" He raised his eyes quickly at the use of the Sioux word for Red Man. "I know what you feel, Pawnee. Oh, don't you suppose I've felt it, too? But it's not love, Pawnee. It's not that, I know!"

"Ye don't know fer me, ma'am," said the breed softly. "Fer me, it's love."

"It's not for me, Pawnee." The girl's words were firming up as she talked, the trembling balance of the emotional moment clearly swinging onto harder ground. "It never had a chance to be. But even if it ever had, it wouldn't now. You said you were going—" She left the words in the air, spreading her hands hopelessly to end them.

"Yeah, I did. Good-by, ma'am. I'm goin' out'n this fort fer keeps. Ye needn't mind gittin' the things, girl. I'll do thet."

Lura's voice was suddenly defiant. "No, Perez! You said ten minutes and I said I'd get them for you. I'll do it. I owe

115

you one, like you said, and that *one* is my life. I'm paying off. I'll be there and I'll have the things. But I want you to know that I've had you wrong all along. And that I'm sorry I said what I did about you to my father and the other officers."

"Whut do ye mean, girl?" the question came with the old, purring quietness. "I don't foller yer track. Ye said somethin' about me to Colonel Clanton?"

"Yes, oh, yes. I was a fool. I told them there was one man in the fort with guts enough to ride this blizzard. To get to Muleshoe Station and telegraph Fort Loring for help. There wasn't a man in the fort who would volunteer to try the ride. I told them you would. I shamed them with you. I even thought right up to a few minutes ago that you meant to go, that that was why you were going for Kentucky Boy. Then when you said you were just getting out of the fort and that was all, I knew how far I'd missed you." The lash of the girl's voice curled back on herself, bitterly. "And I thought I knew men!"

She paused, all the anger gone out of her. When she spoke her voice was toneless. "God forgive me, Pawnee, I thought I knew you."

The half-breed looked at her through an endless silence, the shadow shooting his dark eyes one of rare tenderness. "I thought ye did, too, ma'am," he said, and turned quickly for the door.

The girl's shoulders straightened, her head swinging up, startle-faced, the soft-thrown stone of his statement beginning to widen her eyes with the spreading rings of its implications.

"Pawnee! Oh, Pawnee, I'm sorry!"

But the half-breed's expression had gone dead. Shouldering the guardhouse door open against the hammering blast of the wind, he grunted, gutturally, "Don't fergit the hot water and the whiskey, ma'am. They're fer the hoss."

Perez had never had his hands on Kentucky Boy, but the mare hadn't been in labor with the foal the Pawnee breed couldn't make a kitten of in five minutes. When Lura entered the stall, the big stud was nuzzling the scout as though the latter had bottle-broken him away from his dam's milk-bag.

"I thought this was a bad hoss," the half-breed grinned as Lura came in. "The damn fool's actin' like I'd had him since he quit shovin' his mammy's tits."

"He's a man's horse," said the girl, dumping her burdens in the straw. "You can't fool a horse about a man. They know a

116

man even if some people don't." Her words were humble, Perez not missing their meaning.

"Don't worry about thet, girl. I allow we don't know yet who's right—the hoss or the people."

"I know, Pawnee," her eyes were on him again, "and this time I'll never forget it."

"Ye didn't bring the water," the man ignored her statement and the heating look that swept it toward him.

"It's right here," she said, ducking out the stall door to return with the wooden bucket. "I had to put it down to get the door open."

The breed talked fast, his words as lean as the jaw that housed them. "Dump thet bran in the water and mix it up. Start bucket-feedin' him while I git the saddle on. He'll eat better with somebody holdin' the bucket. He's rotten spoilt."

The girl fed the horse the fragrant bran while Perez cinched the Army saddle, tight up. When he had the girth where he wanted it, he dove under the manger to reappear with two Indian parfleches, a Winchester, two Colts, a long Sioux skinning knife. "My fixin's," he told the girl, shortly. "Had to git them out'n the scout quarters. Run into Murphy on the way out."

"What?" Lura's question wavered, apprehensively.

"We'll have to jump on it. Murphy was jest goin' up onto the north gate fer his guard shift and thet changes things. The north gate's the only one thet I kin git out now, on account the snow's piled so on the east one. And with Murphy watchin' the gate I got to use, thar's some rethinkin' to do. Murphy won't set still fer havin' any whizzer like the colonel's hoss and hat and coat run on him."

"Perez, what are you going to do?"

By this time the scout had laced the parfleches behind the saddle, rammed the Winchester into the scabbard, buckled the Colts on. "Cain't do anything but run a cold bluff. Put the jerky and hardtack in thet left parfleche. Ye got whiskey in thet canteen?"

"Yes."

"How much bran left?"

"He's eaten about half of it."

"Pour a big jolt of whiskey into what's left of the bran, mix it good."

Lura followed his instructions, Perez diving under the manger once again, slipping back out with his wolfskin coat
117

and a heavy canvas bag. As he emptied the bag into the right parfleche, the girl noted the flashing stream of its copper-jacketed contents.

"Courtesy of the 16th U. S. Infantry, Colonel Travis Clanton, commanding." The half-breed's grin was wide-mouthed. "Ye got all thet whiskey-bran down thet hoss, girl?"

Lura nodded, upending the empty bucket to show him. The scout nodded back, coming sliding around under Kentucky Boy's neck, a braided Indian hackamore in his hands. The girl's eyes widened.

"You're not going to ride him with a hackamore?"

"Ma'am, he's got a mouth soft as a baby goat's nose. He could be rode with nothin', but this is jest to let him think he's got a bridle on. I don't want any kind of a bit in his mouth when he starts to breathin' rough."

"Pawnee, how far is it to Muleshoe Creek?"

"Hundred and ninety mile. Why?"

"Do you think he can make it?"

"I allow he kin. If he don't die, meantime. He's the most hoss ever I see."

"Oh, Pawnee, he's so beautiful. I—"

"Don't worry about the hoss, girl. He'll go the distance."

"I didn't mean that, Pawnee. How about you? You're the one that really counts. Can you make it? Oh, Pawnee, do you really think you can? Those poor little kids in that powder mag—"

"Yeah, sure." The scout nodded the interruption. "I reckon if the hoss kin go thet far I kin manage to go with him. Thet is, if I kin keep my hair on."

"You will—oh, Perez, you will!"

"I allow I will. Wouldn't be tryin' it elstwise. I ain't hankerin' to hit the travois tracks fer Wanagi-yata, no more'n the next nigger."

"What's Wanagi-yata, Perez?"

"The Sioux shadowland—the Gathering Place of the Souls."

"You won't get there, not this trip, Pawnee! I know it, here!" Lura pressed her hand to her heart.

The half-breed had turned to check Kentucky Boy. "All right, boy," he soothed the horse, making a last adjustment on the cheek-strap, "now ye got plenty of mouth. Let's make long tracks away from hyar, little hoss. Git the door, girl."

Turning with the words, the scout bumped into Lura Collins standing close behind him, arms half reaching, mouth parted, curvingly.

118

"I said, git the door, ma'am. Time's runnin' out on me."

The girl stood, motionless, her long green eyes sweeping his dark face, her body so close to his the warmth of it came to him even through the deep wolfskin.

"It's running out on both of us, Pawnee." Her voice, lower than a wind whisper in a willow grove, backed the eyes which were burning up at him through the stable gloom with a fierce heat. With the words and the look, the perfume of her came clouding around the bearded half-breed, a dizzying, sudden, female fragrance. It was in his nose. He was tasting it on his lips. It was all through him, raging instantly, running like high phosphorous tides over midnight coral reefs—the nerve-melting animal warmth of pure woman-smell.

"We'll see if we cain't stop it, summat," the phrase came guttural as a bear's growl, the reaching arms with it, cording into her soft back with paralyzing force.

The couch of the clean prairie straw came up around the girl's frantically twisting form like a vast, soft relief, stilling her racing fears, thick-hushing her throaty voice.

"Pawnee, ah, Pawnee-man—"

Sergeant Murdo Murphy sat hunched in the guard hut at the north gate, contemplating the manly rigors of stockade life in the Far West. His watch companion, Corporal Sam "Tennessee" Boone, had just departed kitchenward for another pot of hot Arbuckle's. Alone for the moment, the sergeant, for lack of better company, was talking to himself.

"Faith, now, Murdo me lad, yez had best be composin' yer talk with the Lord. Whut with Father Flannagan down to Fort Lorin' fer the winter, there's no one but yerself to do it. And with them haythin Siouxs squattin' around yez like buffler wolves waitin' fer a sick cow to freeze to death, who else is goin' to administer extrame unction? Nobody, Murdo me lad. Yez had best be thinkin' of yer sins.

"Now, let me see. There was thet Comanche gurl down to Fort Riley last summer—but shure the Lord don't count them haythin conquests. Then there was Moriarity's colleen, but then, faith! I was thet drunk I didn't recognize the gurl till I had her skirt over her head. Ah, Macushla Machree! 'Tis somethin' awful fer yez to be sittin' here, Murdo me bye, with no prayst within two hundird miles and—"

"'Shall we pray, now, Murphy?" The cynical question, coming out of the snow-whirling dark, jumped the sergeant's nerves half an inch out through his freezing skin.

119

"Goddam yer black soul, Perez! Comin' sneakin' in on a man like thet. Why didn't yez knock?"

"Injuns never do," grunted the scout. "Come on, help me git this hyar gate open. I'm goin' out."

"The hell yez are! Whut fer?"

"Colonel Clanton's sendin' me out to try and git through to Muleshoe Creek."

"God in Hivvin, yez don't mean it?"

"Sure, what the hell do ye think he let me out'n the guard-house fer? Good behavior?"

"I dunno. Last I heard he was goin' to keep yez in there till Satan shook hands with Saint Peter."

"Wal, he's changed up his mind summat. It's an old woman's privilege. I'm ridin' out. Come on, put yer shoulder to thet gate, Murphy."

"Ah, well, Perez lad, did the colonel issue yez a pass, now?" The half-breed sensed the crafty change in the voice, tensed accordingly.

"Murphy, ye've slipped yer head hobbles. Do I usually git passed out to go on a scout?"

"This is different, laddie buck. Captain Howell sez nobody cracks these gates to so much as take a piss out'n, without they've got a pass from Colonel Clanton."

"All right, Sergeant," the scout bluffed, "ye wait right hyar whiles I amble back and have the Old Man write ye out my life's history. While he's at it he kin scribble ye a nice, long billy-do about how he loves to scratch out four-page gate-openin' instructions fer hammer-headed company sergeants. I'm certain sure he'll be delighted havin' his dispatch held up while yer touchin' devotion to Captain Howell's orders is plumb satisfied. If I know Clanton, he'll be tickled rosy to find out thet Captain Howell has taken over the command. I'll be right back, Murphy. I—"

"Tch! Tch! Perez, lad. Hold up there. On second thought, maybe yez have a point. The Ould Man ain't in jest the mood to—"

"Ye bet yer ass, he ain't. Let's go!"

"Yes, sir." Murphy was heading for the hut door. "Don't let me detain yez, Mister Perez."

Outside, Murphy put his shoulder to the stockade gate. Glancing around, seeing no mount, he queried, curiously. "Ye're not goin afoot are yez, man?"

"I got my hoss back of the hut, hyar. Ye jest git thet gate apart. Give me about four foot of openin', thar."

"God rest yer soul, bye," Murphy shouted as the wind boomed in through the crack in the opening barrier, "ye'll never make Muleshoe Crick in this weather."

"Not if ye intend standin' thar wobblin' yer big Irish jaw all night," the scout shouted back, bringing Kentucky Boy out from behind the watch hut. "Git the hell out'n thet gate, Murphy. We're comin' through!"

As the scout spoke, the sergeant turned from the opened gate, noticed the horse for the first time. "Wait up, lad," his brogue went soft. "Ain't thet Kentucky Bye ye're leadin'?"

"It ain't his mother," Perez began. "Colonel Clanton give—"

"Colonel Clanton never lets nobody ride thet stud. Ye'll have to git a pass, mister!"

"I've got it right hyar, Murphy." The scout moved easily toward the soldier, reaching inside the wolfskin coat as he went.

"Keep yer hand out of thet coat." Murphy clubbed his carbine, threateningly.

"Whutever ye say, Sergeant." The hand came up and away from the coat with looping speed. Murphy threw up his arms, protectively, but a man doesn't move fast when he's been on watch half an hour with the temperature squatting at 40° below. The Colt barrel flashed into the side of his head with a ringing crack, and Perez stepped back to let the noncom's body slide forward, past him, into the snow.

"Easy, boy, easy—" the half-breed soothed the plunging thoroughbred. "Like as not ye'll see other bodies in the snow this side of Muleshoe Crick."

Swiftly retrieving the sergeant's carbine, slinging it over his own shoulder, Perez wondered what he was going to do about the unconscious Murphy. Left as he was, the sergeant would freeze to death in ten minutes. At the same time Perez couldn't risk taking him back to quarters. As the half-breed hesitated, a looming figure bulked up out of the storm.

"Hey, is thet you, Murphy?"

"Who's there?" the scout parroted the Irish sergeant's brogue.

"Sam Boone. Who the hell was you expectin'? Gen'ril Custah? Whar's the goddam gate? Ah've lost you agin."

"This way, Tinnissee." Perez kept Murphy's thick tongue working.

"Say, Sarge," the corporal shouted back, stumbling toward the sound of the scout's voice, "you ain't seen thet half-breed, have you? He done busted out and stole the colonel's hoss.

Thet hot-lookin' gal of the colonel's he'ped him do it. Stable sergeant caught her comin' out'n Kentucky Boy's stall. He jest herded her into the kitchens as Ah was comin' away with the cawffee."

"Faith, now, Sam, jest kape comin' with thet Arbuckle's. I feel real faint. In fact, me bye," the scout's dark face lit up, "ye'll find me ignarunt body alyin' in the snow where Perez knocked me thick head in. And please close the blastid door after him. The haythin scut has left it wide open behind him, he's thet ill brung-up."

By the time he called the last words, Perez had the horse out the gate. Throwing a last glance back through the narrow opening, he saw Corporal Boone stumble over the prostrate form of Sergeant Murphy, heard him curse as he discovered its identity, waited only long enough to see the tall hill man come running toward the open gate.

Seconds before Tennessee reached the jarred stockade opening, the swirling snows closed behind the rump of Kentucky Boy. The puzzled soldier peered strainingly out into white nothingness. Even as his quick eyes picked them up, the double line of tracks, man's and horse's, leading away from the gates, faded under the shifting drive of the piling snows.

Fifty yards out, Perez began circling the stockade, from the north gate around to the south wall. Here, he turned due south, still leading Kentucky Boy, still stepping each step as cautiously as though it had been high noon of a clear, autumn day.

He did not expect to encounter any hostiles abroad. It was somewhere between 4 and 5 A.M., the temperature hovering near 50° below. The wind which had been screaming crazily for twelve hours had suddenly fallen away to a ghost's whisper. The snow fell straight down.

Perez picked his way, cat-footed, through the whiteness. Every feathery bush and loaded tree branch, the unwary jarring of which might unloose a telltale downslide of piled snow, was fastidiously avoided. Behind the scout, blowing softly, enjoying the bite of the keen snow air in his belling nostrils, Kentucky Boy stepped as gingerly as a buck deer with rank wolf-smell in his nose. This was a new game, very fascinating. Keep your neck stretched out, follow the man in the buckskins and wolf coat. That was apparently the idea.

Perez figured that, next to women, horses were the noisiest creatures in the world. And he knew the surest way to arouse

122

the curiosity of either was to ignore them. The furtive actions of the man ahead of him excited Kentucky Boy's inquisitiveness. His reaching nose hung on the tail of the scout's wolf coat like a Walker or Redbone hound following a fox drag. Horse-wise, the breed never looked back, only clucking softly now and again as the big stud walked up too close on him.

When he had counted a thousand steps south, Perez nose-wrapped the tall thoroughbred, gentling him and whispering to him all the while. Then they went forward again, caution redoubled.

The half-gloom of the coming daylight was beginning to penetrate the blackness of the blizzard and they were getting into a belt of timber at about that distance from the fort where the scout calculated to find the Sioux lodges—if indeed he found them at all.

He had no knowledge of Captain Howell's spotting of the lodge-smokes, had unknowingly placed the location of the tipis almost exactly.

"If we kin git another mile without we walk into somebody's tipi flap," he whispered to the curious thoroughbred, "we kin mount up and make our run fer it."

But the half-breed knew he faced a greater danger than stumbling into the hostile lodges, a danger made vastly graver by virtue of Kentucky Boy being a stud—the Indian pony herd!

The red men always placed themselves between their enemies and their own precious horse herd, hence Perez' certain knowledge that once he got past the lodges, his biggest danger lay yet ahead. Walking into a hare-brained covey of half-wild Indian mounts in company with an eye-rolling stud-horse of Kentucky Boy's evil virility would be about as entertaining as leading a crossbred collie into a cavy of house cats.

The half-breed had no illusions about the prognosis for his trip should any such equine symptom develop unexpectedly. Trying to hang on to thirteen hundred pounds of hot-blooded Kentucky stud, while that brute was simultaneously trying to cover every broomtail Indian mare and kill every scrubby hostile stallion in sight, would add up to a very short ride for Pawnee Perez.

The scout grinned mirthlessly at the thought. Oh, well. With any kind of luck they'd get over the next mile without bumping into either the lodge-line or the pony herd.

As it happened, luck was looking the other way—and so was Perez.

The first warning was an explosive snort from Kentucky Boy, the kind of nose-cleaning blast that always follows a horse getting his first whiff of something he doesn't like.

Perez was under the stallion's neck in an instant, holding the animal's head down, hard. But the damage was done. Off to the right came an answering snort, followed by two or three inquiring whickers. The next moment, a single file of mounted warriors shadowed up through the slanting snows. The braves had apparently not heard Kentucky Boy's snort but were nevertheless on the alert because of the nervousness of their own mounts. They passed so close to Perez he could hear the grunting and breathing of the ponies, the squeezy jingle of the frozen harness, the guttural conversation of the riders.

"I heard something."

"So did I."

"Aye, me too. It was over this way."

"It sounded like a horse."

"It was a buck deer. I know their snort. It was a buck, that's all."

"Wi Sapa is a wise mare. She doesn't whinny at bucks."

"Ha! That mare is stud-crazy. She would neigh at a mouse if she thought he could service her."

"Shut up!" the warning came hissing from the last rider in line, a handsome, dark chief whose black horse now came bulking up out of the snow mists. "Nothing could be heard with you *heyokas* yammering like curs over a string of buffalo guts. Sit still and listen."

The line halted abreast of, and about ten yards out from, Perez' hiding place. The scout held his own breath, Kentucky Boy's nose, Murphy's carbine. Had he had a third, spare, hand, he would have been holding something else—just for luck!

If the half-breed had a God, he was talking to him just then. Very earnestly. Those ponies out there were warm. As they stood, the smoke curled off their gaunt flanks and steamed from their nostrils in spurting plumes. This would mean they had been out on patrol, were returning, that the lodges lay somewhere very close at hand. As if this weren't enough, the snowfall slackened momentarily, letting still more daylight down through the storm, allowing the scout to see the whole line of waiting warriors. For the first time he got a good look at the chief on the black horse, a look that clamped his hard-

124

held breathing yet tighter: Nakpa Kesela, American Horse, the number-three War Chief.

The shock of this revelation, for Perez, lay not in the chief's reputation but in the fact his identity let the scout know what kind of horse he sat. Usually the Indians favored geldings for patrol or war-party work. Mares, if very well trained and not horsing, were sometimes employed, stallions almost never. The latter's eagerness to challenge or court, as the sex of the enemy's mount might dictate, was far too great a hazard for any but a very great warrior.

American Horse was unquestionably a great warrior, and the nervous black brute he bestrode, unquestionably a stallion.

Luck, an iron hand, and the fact that none of the mares in the hostile patrol were horsing had allowed Perez to keep Kentucky Boy quiet up to this point. But if the thoroughbred winded that black stud, a man might as well try to keep a swamp cat quiet on a coon dog's back. Their fat would not only be in the fire, it'd be fried till hell wouldn't have the cinders. The half-breed tightened his hold on the horse's muzzle.

He didn't tighten it quite enough.

American Horse sat his mount for a long twenty seconds. During the silence it seemed to the scout as if the blizzard itself stopped breathing. Finally, the chief put heels into the black, sending him up the line of standing ponies—on Perez' side.

Just before the chief drew even with the half-breed's cover, his deep voice grunted. "*Hopo. Hookahey. Let's go!*" At the same moment his quick-stepping little stallion flirted his arrogant rump a scant six feet from Kentucky Boy's outraged nose.

Hopo? Hookahey? Let's go? Never was command so enthusiastically obeyed. Everything—Indians, mares, geldings, stallions, scout and chief—went at once.

Kentucky Boy bombarded out of that spruce clump showering snow all over hell, including the six nearest Indians. As he went, Perez went with him, fists knotted in the waving mane, long steps catapulting him onto the charging bay's back.

He made no attempt to head the crazed animal, letting him career, full-tilt, into the War Chief's black. Near three-quarters of a ton of grain-fed thoroughbred hit eight hundred pounds of winter-thin Indian pony, massive shoulder to scrawny rump, and the result was inevitable. The squealing

125

black went jughead over flailing heels into the snow, American Horse somewhere in the leg-thrashing mess with him. Kentucky Boy, instead of tarrying to make a fight of it, kept right on going—for a notably sharp reason.

As he had swung up onto the plunging stud, Perez had flashed the long skinning knife from beneath his wolfskin coat. When Kentucky Boy slammed into the Indian pony, the scout slammed the knife into Kentucky Boy; not once, but three, four, five times; the driving blade whipped into the startled bay's rump. The impetus of the stinging slashes carried the big horse squarely over his fallen foe and right on through the scattering line of the hostile patrol.

Not the boy, Pawnee Perez, to linger, monkey-a-horseback, in the middle of a studhorse fight when a keen knife and a hard arm could get him elsewhere. Especially when he had a hundred and ninety miles to ride, and with such a charming farewell committee to speed him on the first lap of it. Turning in the saddle, Perez threw back his head, let out the long-drawn wolf howl that was the victory call of the Pony Stealer People. Behind him, as the bay stallion flattened into his stride, the half-breed could hear the sounds of the gathering pursuit, sounds which were the immediate least of his worries. The Indian pony hadn't been dropped that could catch this big horse under him. After the first fifty jumps, the scout pulled the bay down to a hand gallop.

Definite light was coming now, gray and sick through the blizzard's shroud. This light, moments later, guided him through the sleeping lodges of the Oglala siege lines. A few early-rising oldsters, toting in wood for the morning's cooking-fires, were the only witnesses to the half-breed's dash through the camp. These broke and scattered wildly for the shelter of the nearest lodge and, as the bay cleared the last of the tipis, Perez threw another derisive wolf howl at them.

This was the third time, counting that months-old howl he'd flung at Red Cloud just before the War Chief jumped Lieutenant Collins' sleeping cavalry camp, that Pawnee Perez howled at the Oglala Bad Face Sioux—and it was the last.

The short break in the weather that early morning of the twenty-second closed like a trap behind the half-breed as he left the Indian village.

All that day and the following night he rode south in a freezing blackness which scarcely varied with coming dawn or departing daylight. Twice, he stopped to dry-feed the blowing stallion, carefully rationing him with the rolled oats which mingled with his own hardtack and jerky in the left parfleche.

The second day and night went as the first, and after them, the third day.

That ride of Pawnee Perez', south from Fort Will Farney through the blind gut of a North Plains blizzard, must remain at once and forever a source of pride and mystery to the West. Horses and men will circle in a blizzard, but Kentucky Boy and the half-breed rode a line as straight as a surveyor's chain. Seventy-two hours, one hundred and ninety miles, one horse, one man, no fires built, frozen hardtack and jerky, dry oats and snow, that was the way of it.

Senses are lost in a blizzard and instincts smothered in the careening darkness. Nostrils are riveted shut, eyes, mouth and nose jammed and plugged with frozen snow. And always the incessant yelping and bawling of the wind, screaming at a man, slashing at a horse, buffeting, hammering, pushing, twisting, till the rider's brain is reeling from the sheer noise of it, and the mount is staggering from the relentless force of its constant driving.

No wonder the West still marvels at that ride. By the pure guts of one man and one horse—a sullen man of uncertain pedigree, a blue-blood Kentucky racer with a registered background as long as a lover's good night—the greatest ride in any horseman's history was willed and made. Pawnee Perez and Kentucky Boy! Strange companions, indeed, to blaze one of the wildest of frontier history's forgotten trails. Had Pawnee Perez been a white man you would know his name as you do Custer's or Kit Carson's. But history has no use for half-breeds.

It was the third day. Perez, feeling the dropping bite of the temperature, knew the sun was gone, another night crowding in on him.

Suddenly, through an uplifting swirl of snow, Muleshoe Creek loomed ahead. The scout knew that ford where the Virginia City Road crossed the little stream as you would know your back yard. Beyond it, still invisible behind the sheeting snows, would lie the mud hut and huddled corrals of the telegraph station.

Now was the time for a man to get off his horse and walk softly. If there were any place on the Road better suited for a Sioux trap, Perez couldn't have placed it for you. They would probably have that station covered like a blanket.

127

Still, with the snow as heavy as it was, a man ought to be able to sneak in, all right. Biggest danger would be getting shot at by the jumpy Army troops manning the tiny post.

Perez eased down off Kentucky Boy. They had made it! The thought leaped through him with electrifying warmth. They had broken through Crazy Horse's and Red Cloud's hostiles. They had outsmarted and outrun American Horse and his war patrol. They had lasted out the cold. They had beaten the Indians and the blizzard.

Perez was not a pleasant man, but the grin which cracked the frost-bitten face at the sight of the Muleshoe Crossing was one of rare happiness. Beyond that ford lay fire and food and a warm bed for him; hot bran and a cozy stall for the great horse which trembled so violently beside him. More important: beyond that ford lay the telegraph that would flash the news of Fort Farney's disaster to the waiting troops in Fort Loring, the troops already no doubt alerted by the earlier message which Bailey and O'Connor must have sent, the troops that would come snow-plowing up the Virginia City Road to reach Colonel Clanton's besieged garrison just before their wood and water, and their will, gave out; the troops that would mean the difference of life and death to the strange red-haired girl whose passionate promises to wait for him, given in the panting moments of that wild, crazy stable embrace, had carried the half-breed through miles where no other human will could have done so.

Perez thought only of Lura Collins as he went stumbling down toward that ford. She had made him know a happiness that made the frozen stump of his right foot a mere inconvenience; the frost-dull hands and face, simple injuries to be borne with a short grin and a shrug. She had been his woman and she was going to be his woman. That was the great thing. That had been her promise when he'd left her in Kentucky Boy's stall. And she was a white woman. The white daughter of a white Eagle Chief. With such a woman by his side, he could go any place and look another man in the eye. Another white man in the eye. He would be white, then. That was the wonderful thing. That was all that mattered. That and the unbelievable fact that the girl was a white woman. And that she was waiting for him, Perez, the Pawnee half-breed!

Behind the scout, Kentucky Boy staggered, half-blind with fatigue. Once he stumbled to his knees and would have gone down, but the man was instantly there, holding the horse's

128

head up, clucking to him in an outlandish tongue. "H'g'un, h'g'un! Come on, Boy. Hopo. Hookahey. Owanyeke waste. We're thar, sweetheart. Co-o-o, Boy. Git up. Hun-hun-he! Easy, easy—"

The big stud was up, then, lurching along, head literally on the man's shoulder, eyes glazing, protruding tongue lolling between the yellow teeth.

They were across the creek, going up the far bank. They had made it, man and horse. Perez had the wolf-grin working overtime. Kentucky Boy sensed the triumph rising in the man, perked his halting footsteps in response.

A low hummock of snow appeared in the trail ahead. In avoiding it the scout stumbled wearily, went sprawling, face-down, over a second hummock hidden behind the first.

With tired curiosity, Kentucky Boy reached his head down to sniff at the obstacle which had tripped up his rider. His black muzzle, idly pushing aside the crusted snow atop the mound, became suddenly still. The thin nostrils flared wide as the scent got into them. Uprearing, the stallion lunged back and away from the still, white hummock, eyes rolling in terror, ears pinned, flatly.

Perez, coming up out of the snow in time to observe the stud's spookiness, reached over to brush the snow from the spot the animal had been nuzzling.

The scout's narrow eyes widened a lash-width. Dirty Charlie Bailey had never been the half-breed's idea of a pretty man. Even so, observing him thoughtfully at the moment, Perez decided the other scout had looked much better with his hair on.

There was now no need to question that second mound, but the scout did so, perfunctorily. Beaver O'Connor didn't look any better than Bailey, having been given an even cruder haircut.

That job of trimming was done either in the dark or in considerable of a hurry, mused Perez. A man could see that with half an eye. A generous patch of the dead scout's sandy scalp-lock had survived the lifting to dangle rakishly over his wide-open left eye.

"Sloppy work," commented the half-breed aloud, his professional disgust aroused. "Probably a Cheyenne. Them bastards never did understand thet ye have to cut the damn things loose before ye kin yank them off." Going warily toward the excited Kentucky Boy, the half-breed scout grunted, soothingly, "Whoa, Boy. Easy, easy. *Waste, waste, Sunke Sha.* Easy, now." The big stud whickered softly, getting his ears unpinned, allowing the man to come up to him.

Perez knew now what he would find in the snows ahead of him, this judgment being justified a few moments later as he stood surveying the fire-gutted ruins of Muleshoe Station.

The burned bodies of eight troopers lay twisted among the embers, all but one of the corpses stripped, scalped and mutilated. The left arms of the seven mutilated dead had been severed between the wrist and elbow, identifying the raiders for Perez as the Cheyenne he'd suspected them to be. "Little Wolf and his boys, unless I miss my guess," the scout was muttering half aloud, again. "Wonder why they didn't chop thet eighth soldier?"

Turning the body of the unmarked trooper with the toe of his boot, he had his answer. Suspended around the dead man's neck, its thin chain glinting dully in the fading light, hung a silver crucifix. "*Aii-eee!*" whistled the half-breed. "By God, I was right. Little Wolf, sure as a bitch lobo's got eight tits!"

The chopping off of the left hand or arm was the Cheyenne's tribal trademark; not to be confused with the equally powerful custom of their Sioux cousins—slitting the throat from mastoid to mastoid. By its presence here among the Muleshoe Creek dead, Perez knew the identity of the killers as surely as though he had witnessed the murders. By the same token he could guess the identity of their leader by the respect shown the Catholic soldier. All Plains Indians gave ground to the man who wore a cross, but none of them practiced this regard with the fervor of Little Wolf, the Cheyenne. He was probably the most ruthless butcher among the Cut Arm People, but his personal medicine was the silver cross, and he never took the war trail without first donning the famous, foot-long, argent symbol which was his protective charm.

"I hope ye boys had quit kickin' when ye lost yer fingers," murmured Perez, turning quickly away from the station's charred remains. As he turned, he noted Kentucky Boy gazing curiously at the still forms. Low-voiced, he spoke to the stud, taking the hackamore and backing him quickly into the screening brush away from the burnt cabin. "I told ye ye'd git used to lookin' at bodies in the snow, ye pin-eared bear-bait. Come on, let's us evaporate out'n hyar before them Cheyenne nominates us with a war-ax to run on the same ticket with them boys."

130

Perez put five miles between them and the station, before halting.

Hand-leading Kentucky Boy every step of the way, he disregarded the danger of Indian surprise and the gale force of the blizzard. The half-breed didn't have an ounce of the lard of human sentiment on his lean frame, used his own feet only because he knew the horse's only chance of getting back on his wind was a five-mile walkout. Knew also that the horse was *his* only chance of covering the remaining thirty-five miles to Fort Loring. Without Kentucky Boy to tote him, Perez would become nothing more noteworthy than the third white mound on the trail north of Fort Loring.

The walk took an hour of precious time. But at the end of it, the bay stud's breath had quit sobbing and the scout's frozen right leg had gotten feeling back in it as far as the knee.

He fed the horse the last of the hardtack, poured the remaining whiskey down the beast's throat after the biscuit. Finishing the last few drops in the canteen, himself, he unsaddled the stud, abandoning saddle, ammunition, parfleches, Murphy's carbine, his own Colts. All were quickly cached, the half-breed carefully marking the spot. A man could easily get them again, once he'd made the ride to Loring—if he made it. If he didn't, he'd have damn little use for them in hell.

Carrying only his Winchester and the shells in it, he swung up on the bay, putting him down the trail at the best gait the lead-legged stallion could furnish. Kentucky Boy responded with all the breeding in his deep body, but even as he started he was running rough.

Feeling the off-rhythm pounding of the great heart and the ragged fluttering of the lungs beneath his clamping legs, Perez knew he was riding a dead horse.

A rider in a blizzard casts no shadow. But as Perez began those last miles he had thirty-one shadows trailing him down the Virginia City Road.

Five miles back, at Muleshoe Station, Little Wolf, the Cheyenne, stood with his war party looking down at the fresh tracks of a man and a horse. The still-standing north wall of the post stable sheltered the tracks from the cover of the constantly blowing snow. They led out, south, down the Virginia City Road, before they disappeared in the blindness of the open snows.

Squatting over them, fingering and smelling their depressions, squinting at them intently, a wizened warrior crouched. He was a dwarf of a man, no taller than a short pony's withers,

131

and he was Tonkasha, Red Mouse, best of the Cheyenne trackers.

"*Akicita?*" Little Wolf barked the question.

"No, no soldier," the little man shrugged. "Scout. *Wasicun* scout."

"White scout? How long?"

Again, the withered brave shrugged, "Who can say? It is a cold trail."

"Any smell?"

"Only a little."

"Enough?"

"Possibly."

"Tonight, then. The white scout passed this way tonight?"

"Oh, tonight, sure."

"If his horse is tired we might catch him?"

"Why not? Aren't we *Shacun?*"

"Tonkasha says, 'Why not?'" echoed Little Wolf to the waiting braves. "I say, let's go. Let's go after him. I want his arm." A rolling growl of assent rumbled among the warriors. The ponies, fresh and nervous, jumped eagerly to the hard hammer of the moccasined heels. Within seconds the stark walls of Muleshoe Station stood alone.

The Junior Officers' Winter Ball was the highlight of Fort Loring's social season, a trite expression to be sure, but then it was a trite ball.

Fort Loring had grown up. No longer the dangerous frontier outpost. No longer the sanctuary for the handful of hard-bitten troops fending off the hostile thousands swarming down on the early traffic of the Medicine Road. To be sure, Red Cloud, Crazy Horse and Sitting Bull were familiar names. To be sure, emigrant trains trying to run the forbidden rapids of the Powder River Road still went aground on the dangerous red rocks guarding that disputed channel. But that wasn't Fort Loring. That was days and days away, somewhere up that crazy North Trail. The Virginia City Road they called it, didn't they? Some such name. No matter, anyway. It was outside Fort Loring's world by a million miles —well, anyway, by two hundred and thirty-six miles. What was the difference?

At the moment, 11:30 P.M., December 24th, the big thing was the Junior Officers' Ball.

Everything was going splendidly. Lights, laughter, champagne, dancing, handsome uniformed men, beautiful per-

132

fumed women. The whole, gay panoply of a Christmas Eve military ball shone and echoed through the gleaming windows. What matter that the worst blizzard in a decade was howling down the scratchy efforts of the post musicians? It was Christmas Eve. That was the main thing.

Two hundred and thirty-six miles north, Christmas Eve was coming to another garrison.

There were lights there, too, but only the flicker of the lone stove in the deserted company kitchens. There were women there, but they weren't beautiful and they weren't dancing. They were huddling like clay-faced dolls in the bowels of the powder magazine, awaiting the war-whoops which would mean the Indians were over the stockade and which would signal the explosion which would flash the thick magazine logs to flying splinters.

There were uniformed men there, but they weren't handsome and they weren't laughing. They were shoveling. Shoveling to keep the monstrous drift of the snow from piling to the top logs, shoveling to keep the crouching Sioux from walking over the very top of the stockade on the crest of the rising snow.

Shoveling and cursing and praying. Cursing that none of them had had the courage to ride for help to Fort Loring, that of all men fit to live, the only one who might do so would be the sneaking breed who had led Major Stacey into the massacre and precipitated their whole hopeless situation.

Praying that God, on this his only begotten son's birthnight, might deliver them from the red devil which hovered, waiting, just beyond the blizzard.

And six miles north of Fort Loring, the man they cursed and the delivery they prayed for rode a dying horse down the ice-sheathed North Platte River.

Five miles. Four. And then, three. Two. One. And so, finally, faint through a wind-driven hole in the storm, the lights of Fort Loring.

Twelve, midnight. Intermission. Colonel Gerald Boynton had just danced a Virginia Reel with Captain Swinerton's lovely wife. The entire ballroom was applauding delightedly.

Into the lights, the warmth, the applause, tottered a figure from another world.

Two protesting noncoms put their hands on him as he entered the door. He flung them away from him like an angry bear. Out onto the deserted floor he advanced, lurching, stumbling, almost falling, a monstrous, bareheaded figure in a great wolfskin coat, a frozen, blizzard-borne ghost. From the matted ice of his beard to the caked snow of his buffalo-hide boots, he was an inhuman, unreal apparition.

The women drew back, gasping. The men hesitated, wondering.

The figure in the center of the dance floor stood swaying, arms groping aimlessly like great icy clubs, lean face turning like a death mask, now here, now there, frost-black lips moving soundlessly.

"My God!" a single voice broke the hushed stillness. "The poor devil's blind! He can't see!"

The men surged forward, then, surrounding Perez.

"Good Christ!" breathed a young lieutenant, bringing his hands away from the scout's coat. "His clothes are frozen solid to him."

"Leave his clothes on. Get some blankets and bring him over here on this settee by the stove." Colonel Boynton's orders were terse. A grim-faced captain shoved a flask into the Post Commander's hand.

"Get some of this whiskey down him, sir. The man's dying. Where the hell's Major Johnstone? Johnstone! Major Johnstone!"

The post surgeon surged forward. "Here," he responded, bending over the fallen man. "Hold up, here. Leave him right where he is. Don't get him near that stove. If he thaws too fast, he'll lose his whole face. Looks like the feet and at least that left hand are already gone. Give me that flask." The group watched, wordless, the surgeon continuing to bark his orders. "Coffee. Hot and black. Hurry it up." While he talked, the major was forcing the flask between the frozen man's set lips.

With the whiskey and close-following, scalding coffee, Perez rallied. His eyes flickered open. The cracked lips moved. "Somebody look after thet hoss, outside—"

"All right, old-timer," Major Johnstone reassured him, "we'll get the horse. Here, you, give me that flask again."

One of the noncoms who had followed Perez in spoke slowly as the surgeon poured more whiskey down the scout. "The horse is dead, mister. He's down right where you left him, just outside the door, there."

The half-breed twisted his mouth, spitting whiskey and blood on the floor. "Git away, goddammit. Leave me be. I'm all right, now. Listen—"

134

Harshly, he told them, the words coming haltingly through lips blue-twisted with cold. "Fort Farney's surrounded. Two thousand hostiles. Sioux, Cheyenne, Crazy Horse. They killed Stacey and eighty men. Ambush. Squaw Pine Ridge."

"My God, man!" Boynton was incredulous. "When?"

"Three days ago. Afternoon of the twenty-first."

"Three days! You rode here from Farney in three days? In this blizzard?"

"I'm hyar," said Perez, grimly.

"The hostiles must have gotten the telegraph detail at Mule-shoe?" This from the captain with the flask.

"Little Wolf got it. Everybody killed."

"Flask!" snapped Major Johnstone. "He's going under again—"

"I ain't goin' no place, goddam ye," gritted Perez. "But ye'd best be goin' someplace, Colonel. And thet's up to Farney. They got wood up thar fer mebbe a week, ten days. When thet's gone and the storm lets up, the Sioux'll git them. Mebbe meantime ye kin beat Tashunka to yer friend Clanton."

"God Almighty, man! I can't get a column up to Farney in a week or ten days in this weather."

"Happen ye'd best try," gasped the scout, fighting back the shadows which seemed determined to get between him and his listeners. "They'll hang on fer ye. The Old Man'll fight when he's cornered, and thet How— thet Howell," the half-breed shook his head, forcing the words to come, "he's tougher than a half-boiled buffalo boot."

"He's out again, Colonel," the surgeon spoke flatly as the exhausted man's head sagged. "Let's leave him alone."

"We've got to get him around again." The C.O.'s confusion echoed that of all around him. "We don't know his name, or who the hell he is, or anything. How can we go on his story?"

The surgeon glared at his questioner, started to say something, decided better, seized the scout's shoulders. "Come on, old-timer," he urged, gently, "come around. Who are you? Can you hear me? Who are you, friend?"

The half-breed's lips moved painfully. "John Perez—white scout, Army—16th Infantry."

"All right," Major Johnstone stood up, "that's all. Get this man into bed right here. Wrap him up in blankets. No other heat. Send someone for my bag. Get that coffee hot again. And clear out, all of you. I think this man's earned the right to die in peace and privacy."

The two noncoms picked the unconscious scout up as

tenderly as a child. "Bring him along," ordered the surgeon, pushing the lingering onlookers aside.

A nervous young woman stepped back to let the soldiers through with their pathetic burden. "What a horrible-looking person!" she whispered excitedly to her lieutenant husband. "You'd never believe he was a white man!"

"Looks like a damn breed to me," sniffed the young officer, disinterestedly.

4 WANAGI YATA

The Gathering Place of the Souls

LIKE TRAVIS CLANTON, HIS OPPOSITE NUMBER AT FORT
Farney, Colonel Boynton was, if nothing else, a competent
book soldier.

He got his relief column out of Fort Loring by 4 A.M. of
the morning of Perez' arrival, and on up the Virginia City Road
to Fort Farney in a really remarkable eight days.

Clanton had been out of wood twenty-four hours, the blizzard was dying and the Sioux, not dreaming other troops were
within two hundred miles, or better yet two hundred and
thirty-six miles, were leisurely moving up to begin the savory
work of burning Colonel Clanton's masterpiece to the
ground. They had not, however, gotten much further than
beginning to lob a few lazy, long shots down into the en-
closure from the flanking hills when a scout from Little Wolf
rode in with news of Boynton's amazing approach.

"The Eagle Chief from Fort Loring. Plenty Pony Soldiers.
A sun's journey down there. Plenty Walk-a-Heaps, too. How
many soldiers all together? Oh, just plenty. Really a great
plenty. No need to worry about there not being enough soldiers. Like sycamore leaves in October. At least. *Hopo.* Let's
go. *Hookahey.* Let's get out of here."

On the haunches of this messenger's fagged pony, an Oglala
had lathered in from American Horse, patrolling above Fort
Loring.

The only difference between the Sioux's report and that of

Little Wolf's Cheyenne was the natural one between a Cut Arm dullard and a Throat Slitter poet.

"The Eagle Chief comes. Even now he comes. With the sun on the mountain behind us, he comes. The Pony Soldiers are as many as tick birds around a greenscum buffalo wallow. The Walk-a-Heaps swarm like maggots in a dead dog's belly. There is inestimably more than plenty of both horse and foot warriors. Sycamore leaves were not so many. More like cottonwood leaves in June. Or grass spears south of the Powder in May. The Cheyenne's eyes were bad. His tongue was weak. But he had the right idea, for all that. *Hopo! Hookahey!* Let's all go! Right now!"

Red Cloud knew the rules of war-party poker too well not to see a busted flush when it was staring him in the face. He pulled his Lakota Sioux out, heading back for the Tongue an hour after the word came from American Horse.

Black Shield and his Minniconjou followed suit. White Bull and High-Hump-Back and the Hunkpapa threw in, in turn. Dull Knife had already put his Cheyenne on the trail on the strength of Little Wolf's earlier message.

Even Watangoa, Black Coyote, that craftiest and toughest of the minor War Chiefs, gathered his little band of tall, mahogany-skinned Arapahoe bandits and slipped quietly away. *H'g'un!* Courage to those of you not going. *Wagh!* It is not that Watangoa's heart is bad. He would give anything to stay and slaughter the pale-faced weaklings. But he has just remembered a very important date he had made with his old friend Angyh Pih, Big Foot, the Commanche's only son, to run some elk in the Bayou Salade, the South Park of the Rockies. *Hun-hun-he!*

Tashunka Witko and his six hundred Oglala Bad Faces hung on alone, departing only when the morning of January 2nd brought the early sun flashing off the carbine barrels of Boynton's cavalry, six miles down the Virginia City Road.

Fort Will Farney was saved. But the strange, dark-skinned man who had saved it lay motionless on a hospital cot in Fort Loring, face pallid, eyes closed, gray lips still.

If he breathed, the covering sheet gave no sign that he did.

The bulk of the report was a foot long and, to a man with mental guts enough to grind up such terms as "total pedal atrophy, left terminal," and "desiccation, left manual, partial," no doubt very digestible. But any man, even a half-breed scout, could chew up the line that closed off all the medical la-di-da. It was that simple it didn't take a man over twenty minutes of figuring, finger-tracing, mouth-screwing and tongue-biting to get it straight in his head. Finally, it came out: "Discharged. Partial disability. Limited service."

Perez, sitting fully dressed on the side of his hospital cot, handed the paper back to Major Johnstone with a wry smile and no comment.

"How do you feel, Perez?"

"All right. I couldn't fight no bear."

"You'll improve."

"Likely. Whut'd Colonel Clanton say about my job?"

"Well, he's not going to be at Fort Farney for a while, and—"

"Thet don't make no difference. He'll know who is goin' to be thar. Whut'd he say about me scoutin'?"

"Pawnee, I had to tell him about the disabilities. They're so damn obvious. I could have left them off my report but it wouldn't have meant anything."

"Yeah, I reckon. Anythin' else?"

"Sergeant Murphy's downstairs with a horse and outfit for you."

Perez stood up, wincing as his withered foot touched the floor. The surgeon stepped forward. "Here, Pawnee, let me help you—"

"Not quite, medicine man," gritted the scout, pulling away. "I allow I kin stump it. Leastways I got to start learnin'."

"You should have let me take it off," Major Johnstone eyed the twisted limb resentfully. "The damned thing is useless. That God-awful left hand, too. Neither one of them worth a cent for anything."

"Ye talk like a white man, Doc," Perez grinned. "Ye fergit an Injun gits on his pony from the right side. All I need of this left leg is jest to peg me aboard, oncet I git on. As fer the hand, I'm savin' thet fer a friend whut collects them."

"A friend who collects desiccated left hands?"

"Oh, he don't give a crap whether they're dessycated or otherwise. He'll take them in any condition, jest so they're left ones."

"Now, who in the hell," the surgeon responded, curiously, his simple man's suspicion aroused, "would go around collecting left hands?"

"Oh, any Cheyenne, Major, but I'm savin' this one fer Little Wolf. I allow he'd admire the way she's shriveled up and curlycued. He's a connysewer."

Outside the building, Murphy greeted the half-breed effusively.

"Perez, my bye! It's good to see yez. Though, faith, I wouldn't have known yez but fer them Satan's whiskers, ye're thet skinny drawed-out. Whut's happened to yez, lad?"

"Whut's happened to ye, Murphy?" The half-breed eyed him steadily. "'I've bin in thet meathouse near on to a month and nobody but Tennessee's bin close to me. And he wouldn't say nothin' about ye nor nobody else. Whut the hell's goin' on around hyar thet a man's got to be treated like he'd tooken a dose of the clap or somethin'?"

"Ah well, now, Perez man"—the old soldier looked at the ground, shifting his heavy boots uneasily—"lots of things have happened. In me own case, lad, I've taken me a widdy woman, ye'll remember me discussin' her charms? Moriarity's colleen? Ah, yes. Well, bye, yez know how 'tis with them widdied females. A man can't git too much of them and they can't get enough of a man. I've bin—"

"Congratulation, Murphy. Whut's this I hear about Colonel Clanton leavin' Fort Farney? Did he git bustid?"

"Aye, lad, thet he did. 'Tis a cryin' shame, but thet's the way the Army works."

"It's a lousy way. Clanton wasn't to blame fer thet massacre. Goddam the Army. They make a hero out of an idiot like Stacey and cut the guts out'n a good man like the colonel."

"Yez should know, lad. Ye've had nothin' but a sorry time of it from the Army, yerself."

"Thet ain't nobody's fault but my own. I went lookin' fer the job, I allow. I bin bustin' my red ass fer ten years tryin' to be a white man. Thet ain't the Army's doin's. I jest gotten it in my hard haid to turn myse'f white or die tryin'. And I guess I damn near did. Leastways the Doc says I ain't got no business bein' alive. What about Mrs. Collins, Murphy?"

The question, tacked carelessly onto the half-breed's references to the Army, caused the sergeant's red Irish face to bloom like a ponderosa. "Uh, the gurl? Shure now, she's foin. Everybody pattin' her on her pretty back and tellin' her whut a wonderful thing it was fer her to git ye to make thet ride—"

"Murphy—!" the breed lurched toward the cavalryman, his black eyes pin-lighted with sudden intensity. "Goddam ye, don't fun with me. Did she say thet? Thet she got me to do it? Is thet whut she's sayin', Murphy? Thet she fiddled me into makin' thet ride?"

140

Murphy backed off, abruptly. "Now, wait a minute, Perez. It wasn't jest like thet, lad. Ye mistook me. She's a nice enough gurl, I suppose. She probably meant nothin' atall by her talkin'. Why—"

The half-breed's voice dropped back to walk on its old quiet Pawnee moccasins. But there was heaviness in the tread, for all its careful placing of the words. "Quit stallin', Murphy. Whut is it ye're coverin' up? Somethin' about her, ain't it? Whut's she done?"

"Shure, 'tis nothin', now. I wouldn't give it another thought."

"Wal, give it another one," the voice was flat as the cock of a Colt's trigger. "Right now!" The fire-spark shooting the dark eye gave Murphy his warning, but the heart of the Irish was never as hard as the fist.

"Aye, lad," the old sergeant's tones were miserable. " 'Tis jest thet she's bin shinin' them green eyes of herz at the C.O., here, and—"

"Boynton?"

"The colonel, yes."

"Wal?"

"Father Flannagan is marryin' them roight after the review this mornin'. I'm sorry, bye. Yez would have me tell yez. It's why Tinnissee wouldn't talk to yez and it's why I couldn't bring meself to come visitin' yez."

"It's all right, Murphy," the scout's voice was soft, again. "Anythin' else?"

"Yes, lad. I almost fergot. Missus Collins give me this note fer yez."

Perez took the envelope, shoving it, unopened, into his hunting shirt. "Thanks, Murphy." The half-breed turned away, taking the reins of the sleepy-eyed cavalry gelding. "I'll give yer regards to Red Cloud."

The sergeant stood looking after the scout, all the sympathies bred into his Hibernian pedigree for the man who has lost a good heart to a hard maid following him. Presently he remembered something else he'd forgotten to tell the half-breed.

He panted up to the limping Perez, his blue eyes wide with importance. "Faith, now, yez ain't leavin' the fort, Pawnee lad?"

"Not any sooner than I kin possibly do it. Why fer ye ask?"

"The saints fergive us, I almost fergot whut Colonel Clanton sent me to tell yez in the first place!"

141

"Sech as?"

"Well, yez can't leave, yet, lad. Yez have to wait fer the review."

"The hell ye say!" The half-breed's grin was as thin as scum-ice in November. "So Colonel Clanton's a busted hero and they're givin' him the chancet to watch them wave him a techin' farewell. Murphy, ye kin tell the Old Man good-by fer me. I allus liked him and he treated me near white. But fer this damn review, ye kin tell him to stuff it up his butt with a hot needle."

"It ain't *his* review, bye," the Irish sergeant spoke with all his soft mother brogue. "It's yerz."

Perez stood, motionless, the meaning of the old soldier's statement flooding through him. Murphy's voice continued, gently, the patience of the scarred campaigner for his injured fellow-in-arms patent in each careful syllable. "Ye're the hero, lad. And there's not a man of us which stood to them top logs at Fort Farney and shoveled, or which kneeled to them rifle-slits and prayed, whut don't know it. And there ain't a one of us which don't God-bless yez fer it."

The half-breed raised his head. When he looked at Murphy, his black eyes were charcoal-dry. "I'm no hero, Murphy. I made the ride to show Clanton and the rest of ye thet a half-breed could do somethin' thet had all the rest of ye layin' on yer damn yeller bellies and pukin'." The scout's voice was tired, no longer bitter. "And I done it because a white girl laid in the straw with me and told me she would wait fer me."

The pause, then, was the kind that stands awkwardly around when two simple men have trod about as far out on the swampcrust of inner thinking as they dare. The half-breed ended it, abruptly. "I'm goin' back to my people, Murphy. I've tried to walk in the *Wasicun* tracks but I ain't bred to it. My toes keep turnin' in. The prints don't match. Now I'm goin' home to the *Shacun*, if they'll have me. Fer ten years I've tooken my best shots at bein' 'Perez.' *Nohetto!* It's got me nowhars. From hyar on, I'm bein' somethin' I kin. Now, I'm goin' to be 'Panani.' To ye, Murphy," he finished, softly, "thet's 'Pawnee.'"

The sergeant put his bear's-paw hand on the scout's thin shoulder. "Perez, lad, Colonel Clanton's writ to Washington about yer ride. The Guv'mint has sent yez a citation, voted regular, in the Congress itself. There's also a generous cash reward of money bin sent along, to boot. We'd all take con-

142

sid'rable pride in seein' yez git whut's owin' to yez. Yez shouldn't ride out on us, Pawnee bye."

Perez gave in to the humble sincerity of Murphy's appeal. "All right, old-timer. Whut time is the review?"

"Ten-thirty. Thet's jest less'n an hour."

"I'll be thar. Ye kin tell Clanton."

"Thank yez, lad. We're every one of us thet proud of yez!"

The scout limped around the corner of the hospital barracks, the gaunt cavalry gelding trailing him. Presently Perez found what he sought, a deserted place along the west fort wall, where he could have the morning sun warming his shaking, stiffened joints.

Squatting awkwardly down, one knee first, like an old squaw with the bone misery, he eased his weary back against the rough logs, reached inside his shirt, brought forth the envelope, sat looking at it a long time.

When at last he opened it, he studied the writing with a deep frown and the occasional aid of an underlining finger. His lips moved, slowly, framing each difficult word:

"Dear Pawnee,

"I'm asking you to forget everything that went between us. In return, I promise I shan't ever forget any of it. Colonel Boynton and I are going to be married today, after your review. Oh, Pawnee, we're all so real proud of you! I'll be there today and I want you to look at me. I want to know that 'your heart is good for me.'

"You'll always be remembered by 'your girl.'
                                          "Lura Evalynn Clanton"

The scout reread the letter three times, each time turning it to the blank, back side, as though to discover some overlooked postscript. Finally, he replaced the paper in the envelope, folding and refolding it carefully.

An inquisitive snow bunting hopped perkily toward the silent human being seated against the stockade wall. The half-breed eyed the bird, thoughtfully calculated the range, decided it was too long, waited patiently for it to shorten.

Presently it did. The quid of light-leaf Burley shifted speculatively from one angular cheek to the other. With wind, light, range and target just so, Perez spat. The thin stream's trajectory was as flat as a war arrow's flight.

143

Splat! Dead on. Not a drop wasted.

The little bird cheeped shrilly, shook its splattered head, hopped indignantly away.

"Let thet be a lesson to ye," admonished the scout, laboriously hunching himself erect. "Never trust a half-breed."

Picking up the trailing reins of his horse, he added, tightmouthed, "Nor a woman, neither."

Infantry, cavalry, band and color guard wheeled and turned in the muddy slush of Fort Loring's vast parade ground. A big review was no common doings, especially a full-dress turnout like this, and the last soul in the fort was present to give it an eye.

Perez, side by side with Colonel Clanton, fronted the honor group. Behind them, Captains Howell and Tendrake sat their horses. And behind the captains, the silent ranks of the heroes of Fort Farney held their proud braces.

On the far side of the parade yard stood another silent group: the women and children who had spent that terrible week in Fort Farney's powder magazine. Heading this group, red hair gleaming in the morning sun, Lura Collins waited poised and breathless.

Still another gathering watched the wheeling garrison troops of Fort Loring. Rank on blanket-wrapped rank, they squatted; the stony-eyed Agency Sioux, the tame red brother, the eater of the *Wasicun*'s spotted buffalo, allowed to witness this flexing of the white man's military muscles as a fit reward for their adherence to the miserable terms of their slavery.

The final, smallest group on the parade yard impressed even the Sioux.

Ten paces in front of Colonel Clanton and Pawnee Perez, Sergeant Murdo Murphy rigidly presented the colors of the 16th U. S. Infantry and the Fourth Cavalry. Behind Murphy, Corporal Sam Boone, equally rigid, held the slack reins of three borrowed cavalry horses. The horses alone stood at ease. There was no reason to look alive when all that was being borne was empty, black-draped saddles.

Woyuonihan! Wagh! Wait a minute, you horses. Those saddles may be empty but the names that went with them will be long remembered, bravely enshrined: Major Phil Stacey. Captain Winslow Benson. Second Lieutenant Barrett Drummond.

Perez, looking at all this, was seeing only the girl across the

144

field, there, her red-gold hair loose in the wind, her full-curving figure graceful as a doe's.

Colonel Clanton's speech was concise. He praised the heroism of the men and women at Fort Will Farney, lauded the courage and hallowed memory of Major Stacey, commended the hardihood of the scout John Perez and, in the same breath with his reference to the latter, included a eulogy on the heart and breeding of Kentucky Boy, together with his sincere thanks to Colonel Boynton for the use of the field.

After that, he called Perez forward, quickly handing him the long, yellow envelope.

In a quiet that was thick enough to slice with a spade, the half-breed took it, holding it uncertainly for a moment. The envelope bore no seal, no address, but he'd been told it carried within it the official commemoration of his ride, actually *voted* to him, Pawnee Perez, by the Grandfather's Government in Washington. No wonder the half-breed hesitated.

Watching him, Colonel Clanton had no more stomach for this moment than did the confused Pawnee scout. And where Perez was uneasy because he *didn't* know what was in the envelope, Colonel Travis Clanton was upset because *he* did.

"Go ahead, man," the officer's smile spread awkwardly, "it's yours."

The scout, withered left hand hanging, useless, fumbled at the unsealed packet with his good right, finally getting it clumsily open. Inside were three one-hundred-dollar bills. Nothing else.

"Congratulations, Perez! And good luck. Now, about that money, man, I know it—"

"Sure, I know. Don't worry about it none, Colonel," somehow the grin had the old, summer-lightning flash. "It's better than a poke in the eye with a sharp stick."

In the silence that trod the heels of his remark, Perez turned his horse across the field.

"The poor devil!" Captain James Howell's suppressed curse went to his companion, Tendrake. "It's a damn rotten shame."

"There was three hundred dollars in that envelope," shrugged the other, unfeelingly. "Probably more money than he ever saw in one piece. He'll go on a half-breed high-lonesome, get himself screwed by some syph-ridden squaw and wake up thinking he's had one hell of a time."

Howell's sneer would have scorched a softer face. "Three
145

hundred dollars for a man's hand and foot! For saving hundreds of white lives! For robbing the Sioux and Cheyenne of the biggest victory they ever dreamed of! God Almighty!"

"Hell, I can add to your righteous indignation," Tendrake troweled on the mortar of his scarcasm. "Two hundred dollars of that money is back pay he had coming for scouting up at Farney. The Government authorization was for one hundred dollars. I drew the vouchers myself."

Howell's answer was to raise his right hand in stiff salute after the departing scout.

"Now, what the hell was that for?" queried Tendrake, irritably.

"That," his companion muttered, slowly, "was for the bravest man I ever saw—white or half-white."

Pawnee Perez had ridden into the short history of Fort Will Farney alone. He rode out of it the same way.

His departure from Fort Loring was as unattended as had been his arrival. Even the weather, conspiring to set the stage of similarity, sent a lead-gray snow front crawling suddenly over the Big Horns to pile up ominously behind the low flanks of the Laramies. The bright morning sun of the parade ground was snuffed out like a pinched candle.

Corporal Sam Boone stood on the low stoop of Mrs. Lura Collins' quarters, hunching his shoulders to the building wind, stomping his big feet against the creeping cold. The door opened to his hesitant knock, his words stumbling all over themselves getting out of his hung-open mouth. "Uh, beg pardon, ma'am. Uh, Ah'm Sam, uh, Tennessee, Corporal Boone, thet is. Friend of Pawnee's, ma'am. He give me this envelope to bring you-all."

"Please come in, Tennessee." The girl took the envelope, standing aside for the soldier. "Is Mr. Perez going to leave the fort soon?"

"He's done a'ready left, ma'am."

"Oh, no! In this storm?"

"It ain't much of a storm, ma'am. Not to him. He's rid worse ones, I 'low." The lanky corporal looked at the girl openly.

"Yes, he has, Tennessee." The green eyes dropped. "I know."

"I guess you do, ma'am," Tennessee agreed, uncomfortably. This woman was a real creamy cat. The kind any man thought about with other than what God stuck on his shoulders. She made Tennessee want to get out of there, quick.

"Ma'am, Ah—"

146

"I wanted to see him," she interrupted, her words as soft as the beckoning mouth which framed them. "He left the parade yard so suddenly. I tried to get his attention but he wouldn't look at me. He wouldn't look at anybody, Tennessee. What ails him? Do you know?"

"No, ma'am, Ah don't. Them half-breeds carry on queerer'n a slough coon. Like as not yo're right, though. Somethin' was eatin' him."

"You say you were his friend, Tennessee. Didn't he say anything to you?"

"Wal, ma'am, he didn't have no real friends, 'ceptin' thet othuh scout, Hawk Creighton. Thet's the one thet was kilt by Crazy Horse. Otherwise, I 'low it was jest me and Murphy knew him at all."

"But he didn't say anything?"

"No, ma'am. Not about you, iffen thet's whut you-all mean. But he come and see me and Murphy aftuh the review. Give each one of us a hundred-dollar bill. Then he ast me to bring thet envelope ovuh to you. Thet's all. Mebbe you-all had best look in it, ma'am."

Lura Collins nodded, her manner abstract. "He was such a strange man, so bitter." The long fingers opened the envelope. "He always made me feel so uncomfortable—"

"He made a lot of us feel like thet, Missus Collins. It was his way, Ah reckon."

"No—" The tall mountaineer thought the girl's words fell softer than snowflakes on a horse's winter coat. "That wasn't his way, Tennessee. I didn't know until today what his real way was—how he really makes you feel." She paused and the quick eye of the hill man caught the flash of the tear as it fell. "Oh, Tennessee, he makes you feel *ashamed*!"

"Ah've got to go, ma'am. Ah got no business bein' in heah. Ah—"

"Tennessee, wait." The envelope was open now, the girl's eyes staring, startled, into it. "Why, there's nothing in here at all. Just a blank piece of paper. Not a word of writing on it. I don't understand—"

"Ah do, ma'am. About the writin', Ah mean." The big Southerner's drawl was apologetic. "Pawnee, he couldn't write. Ah know thet, ma'am."

Perez rode the out trail five miles, then turned north across country. There was a short-cut away from the treeless valley of the Platte which cut ten miles off the regular route to

147

Muleshoe Station. And if he was going to get up there where he'd cached his guns and outfit, ahead of nightfall, he'd have to hump it.

As he hit the cut-off, the rolling grayness from the Big Horns shut in on him, the first big flakes of the new snow slanting fat and wet into his squinting face.

All afternoon he rode north, the snow setting in heavier all the while, the temperature dropping steadily. By 4 P.M., nearing the cache, the weather had come down hard and Perez, slumped and shaking in the saddle, was a sick man.

Twice along the trail he had stopped and vomited, the second sickness bringing nothing but thin yellow gall flecked with scarlet. For an hour, now, he had been coughing, deep, lobar barks which left his chest aching, his body wringing wet.

Wiping his mouth after the last paroxysm, twenty minutes back on the trail, the back of his hand had come away smeared with bright, bloody mucus.

Nor was it the scout's wasted body, alone, that was sick.

The past two hours his nerves had been going. Every normal trail sight had had his reflexes jumping crazily. Now it was a snow-draped juniper, looming around a turn, sending him spasmodically kicking his horse off the trail and into the underbrush; now a brown cottontail, snow-bombing out of a hummock of bunch grass, starting him in a wild dive for the Winchester under his knee.

Since leaving the Platte Trail outside Fort Loring, he'd been unable to shake the feeling that he was being followed. Again and again he'd doubled back to lie along his own trail. Nothing had come. Not a twig crack. Not an owl hoot. Not a pony whicker.

Finally, he knew there was nothing there. Only wind, and snow, and loneliness. And nerves.

That had been hours ago, before the coughing and vomiting had begun really to tear at him. He hadn't been sick, then. Now, he knew he *was* sick; knew the things he thought he heard were only shadow-sounds jumped up by the twisting sickness that was in him.

For the first time in his life Perez fought fear, the empty, frantic dread that comes up in a strong man when the ferrous vein runs out of nerve ore that has never graded less than pure iron.

That snuffle off there to the right wasn't a pony. That queasing creak wasn't a frozen saddle squeaking. That changing

148

form up ahead wasn't a mounted brave waiting motionless back of the shifting snow screen.

The half-breed ground his teeth, forcing his hand to stay away from the Winchester. Cursing his weakness, he kneed the cavalry horse on forward, into the clearing across which his cached weapons lay. He was out in the open, then. Into the clearing. Where he *could* see.

And that changing form up ahead *was* a mounted brave waiting behind the snow!

The half-breed's horse stopped, nostrils flaring, ears flicking. Perez sat him quietly, head sunk forward, shoulders hunched. The dark eyes, dull with fever, were still bright enough to recognize an old friend.

"*Hohahe,*" said American Horse. "Welcome to our tipi. We've been waiting for you."

Around him now, the scout could see the others, ghost warriors sitting phantom ponies, gray and unreal in the uncertain twilight: Elk Nation, Short Bear, Crazy Lodge, High-Hump-Bear, Bob-Tail-Bull; old friends, all. He did not need the darting glance over his hunching shoulder to tell him of the others waiting there behind him. The dull glow of the foot-long silver cross hung its image in the tail of his eye: Little Wolf, the Cheyenne, was back there. And Tonkasha, the Little Red Mouse, grinning at his chief's side. And the shadowy backing of a dozen others.

"*Woyuonihan,*" Perez returned American Horse's greeting, touching his withered left hand to his brow in the courtesy gesture. "*Wolakota.* I am here in peace. *Hun-hun-he.* I have come home to my people."

"*Hohahe,* welcome home!" barked Little Wolf, and shot him in the back.

The scout stiffened, half turning in his saddle to face the Cheyenne. "*H'g'un!*" The Oglala courage-word somehow beat the belch of dark blood out of the slack mouth.

A dozen mushrooms of black-edged orange bloomed around the clearing's border. The sound of the lead whacking into the half-breed's body shaded the flat reports of the rifles by a half-second. Perez' right hand slid nervelessly into his coat front, hesitated, fell away, tight-closed.

The cavalry mount, unconcerned with the shooting, began walking interestedly toward American Horse's whickering stallion. Perez' body lurched twice to the shifting withers, slid off the right side of the horse, dragged a few feet in the stirrup,

149

broke loose, flopped over to lie still, half covered in a low snowbank.

The Indians were around him, then, dismounted. Little Wolf seized the half-breed's left arm, partially pulling his body out of the snow, his broad scalping knife flashing upward.

A tall shadow fell between the Cheyenne and the dead scout. Little Wolf turned angrily as the restraining hand of the Sioux chief closed on his upraised arm.

"Tashunka Witko has said no." American Horse nodded, soberly. "Tashunka said it was a great ride. He said, no cutting. He said, leave him his hands to guide his pony on the long trail. Tashunka said that. He said, let Little Pony Stealer ride into Wanagi Yata with both hands on the reins. That's all."

"Did he say the hair, too? Did Tashunka say to leave that, too?" demanded the Cheyenne chief, defiantly.

"He didn't say about the hair," shrugged the Sioux.

Little Wolf's knife whipped downward almost before American Horse had spoken. With a snapping jerk the Cheyenne flung the scalpless body from him, kicking it backward with a propelling shove of his knee. The limp figure went into the bank with enough force to bring a showering cover of snow down from an overhanging spruce. When the fall ceased, only the right arm of the scout remained visible.

"The hand was no good, anyway. All curled up!" snapped Little Wolf. "*Hopo*, let's go!"

"*Hookahey*," agreed American Horse. "Let's all go. It's getting cold."

The wind moved in on the heels of the departing ponies, the piling snows beginning their merciful work of covering the last sign of the body under the spruce. A whirling groundgust, smoking across the surface of the snowbank, spun around the exposed hand, tugging peevishly at the crumpled bit of paper in the stiffening fingers.

A second or two and the paper was almost free. Another second and it was rolling across the frozen ground of the clearing, a skittering, walnut-sized ball of crinkly green. Against the root-tangle of a misshapen sage bush it caught, lodging securely.

The last snowy breath of the thieving gust followed in, quickly, burying the hundred-dollar bill almost before it stopped rolling.

LOUIS L'AMOUR
1

BANTAM'S #1
ALL-TIME BESTSELLING AUTHOR
AMERICA'S FAVORITE WESTERN WRITER

☐	13561	THE STRONG SHALL LIVE	$1.95
☐	12354	BENDIGO SHAFTER	$2.25
☐	13881	THE KEY-LOCK MAN	$1.95
☐	13719	RADIGAN	$1.95
☐	13609	WAR PARTY	$1.95
☐	13882	KIOWA TRAIL	$1.95
☐	13683	THE BURNING HILLS	$1.95
☐	14013	SHALAKO	$1.95
☐	13680	KILRONE	$1.95
☐	13794	THE RIDER OF LOST CREEK	$1.95
☐	13798	CALLAGHEN	$1.95
☐	14114	THE QUICK AND THE DEAD	$1.95
☐	14219	OVER ON THE DRY SIDE	$1.95
☐	13722	DOWN THE LONG HILLS	$1.95
☐	14316	WESTWARD THE TIDE	$1.95
☐	14227	KID RODELO	$1.95
☐	14104	BROKEN GUN	$1.95
☐	13898	WHERE THE LONG GRASS BLOWS	$1.95
☐	14411	HOW THE WEST WAS WON	$1.95

Buy them at your local bookstore or use this handy coupon for ordering:

Bantam Books, Inc., Dept. LL2, 414 East Golf Road, Des Plaines, Ill. 60016

Please send me the books I have checked above. I am enclosing $_____
(please add $1.00 to cover postage and handling). Send check or money order
—no cash or C.O.D.'s please.

Mr/Mrs/Miss_____

Address_____

City_____ State/Zip_____

LL2—1/81

Please allow four to six weeks for delivery. This offer expires 7/81.